BEST
WOMEN'S
EROTICA
2012

BEST
WOMEN'S
EROTICA
2012

Edited by

VIOLET BLUE

Published in the United States by Cleis Press, Inc., 2246 Sixth Street, Berkeley, California 94710.

Printed in the United States.
Cover design: Scott Idleman/Blink
Cover photograph: Maciej Laska/Getty Images
Text design: Frank Wiedemann
First Edition.
10 9 8 7 6 5 4 3 2 1

Trade paper ISBN: 978-1-57344-755-3
E-book ISBN: 978-1-57344-772-0

"Drought," by Olivia Glass, first appeared in *Filament Magazine*, Issue 8 (June 2011).

CONTENTS

INTRODUCTION:
A FINE SMUTTY ROMANCE

Just before working on this edition of *Best Women's Erotica*,
I was interviewed by an MFA lit class about erotica, erotic
anthologies and specifically, *Best Women's Erotica 2011*. The
students were surprised that the stories in this popular little
anthology were not classic porn writing, nor were they traditional romance. They seemed perplexed that it was literate smut
they were reading, which by its nature ought to be far from
love and happy endings. What on earth, they wanted to know,
was this sought-after hybrid of literate erotic fiction, and what
makes it tick?

I wondered if this question came from a perception that erotic
writing for women must include romance—and its doppel-
ganger, porn writing with explicit sex, must not. And never the
two shall meet—well, that's how it used to be, anyway. I think
this is a common assumption, but not here, and not anymore.
The truth is, what I've found in erotica is that what women
want from their "bodice-rippers" is far more interesting than
the simple equation of porn versus romance.

The widely held perception the students brought to a book

labeled "erotica" and yet marketed to women was that there must be a trend away from romance. They asked me, is it that women don't want "happily ever after" anymore? No, I explained. It's that we want hot sex *and* sublime romance, thank you very much, and we don't feel like apologizing about it anymore. Also, as you'll see in this edition of *Best Women's Erotica,* each woman's vision of romance is as unique to her as her tastes in sexual adventure are.

Not to mention that current erotic romance as a genre has undergone a serious transformation in the past ten years. The trend is not necessarily away from romance, but it's also no longer required—though desire always drives our erotic heroines' hearts, minds and bodies. The stories here reflect the cutting edge of this transformation, where there is more sex, less apology for wanting it, and strong, self-actualized characters.

The lack of apologetic female characters in *Best Women's Erotica* will surprise you. In fact, this edition is full of surprises. If you compare this collection to a more traditional collection of racy reads for women, the female protagonists in those volumes always seem to need an excuse for sexual desire. Those stories are often given titles like "The Birthday Gift" or "Day Pass." It's like they all have to get some sort of permission for the sex they want, as in, there is always some reason outside of the fact that *they really want it.*

The women in these stories are driven by desire: physical, emotional, and occasionally erotically fueled intellectual curiosity. In this, the genres of smut and romance are no longer diametrically opposed, but now work in concert to give us everything we want, and more. Even if sometimes, like a few of the women in these stories, what we want is kinky and taboo.

We also want realistic sex, believable stories and real characters—on top of that, we don't want the scene to fade out when the sex begins. High erotic tension, risk and reward, something unpredictable and inspiring—we want women at the center of pleasure. And for me, as the editor and a devoted erotica reader and fan, each story has to be unforgettable. I want to wish I were there, in each and every story; each should be a tale so riveting and smart and layered and filthy I want all my friends to read it as soon as possible.

And I want my friends to read every single story in *Best Women's Erotica 2012*.

In "Drought," by Olivia Glass, a woman becomes stuck in highway traffic on a wetly hot afternoon, thinking about the man she left asleep in her bed. She surprises drivers as she takes matters into her own hands, as she relives the hot sex she has every time her man comes over and tears off his suit.

Louise Lush's "Tweetup" is a delightfully arousing and playful tale of a woman who tweets about porn and her pet frogs, then attends a meetup only to end up in bed with her favorite tweet-flirt, with rapturous results. "Eddie's All-Night Diner," by K. D. Grace, is the ultimate clandestine dining frisson. In it, a woman who frequents an all-night diner to secretly watch other couples engaged in sexual flirtation is approached by a big hot guy who obviously knows what she's up to—and silently challenges her limits of sexual daring in the middle of the restaurant.

In "Pleasure's Apprentice," by Remittance Girl, a college dropout goes to work in a silver shop and becomes party to tense sexual encounters with an older man who instructs her in silver—and sex. They never talk; she learns to polish silver and have dirty, dominated sex, until she leaves a year later. "The Nylon Curtain," by Elizabeth Coldwell, features a quirky, sexy and happy ending after a young woman with plans of writing a book about her experiences of Internet sex trawling agrees to meet a man with a vintage stocking fetish. When the '40s-era stockings and garters push her own arousal buttons, she pushes his farther than he's prepared to go, with unexpected results.

Rosalía Zizzo's "A Big Deck" is all about what happens when a woman who plays poker with a group of men teases the main player about his "big deck"—resulting in a riveting, satisfying performance of oral sex in front of the other guys. "Bad," by Kay Jaybee, is fraught with daring as a woman involved with a kinky guy has to decide just how bad she's willing to be when he phones her up and challenges her to do naughty stuff with another woman while he watches.

Amelia Thornton's "Dolly" is the most controversial of the selections; in it a woman's role-play Daddy has gotten her a life-sized Dolly—a woman playing a consensually submissive mannequin—and she sits in her playroom smacking the dolly first with her hand, then with a hairbrush and much more. In "No Rest for the Wicked," by Jacqueline Applebee, a woman turned on by fear and danger meets a guy at a friend's wedding party, and when she gets him back to her room, at her urging he becomes the scary, knife-wielding tough guy she hoped he'd be.

A cheeky female poet stars in "The Skin Doctor," by Tsaurah Litzky, where a doctor's visit pairs her woman-centric-poet principles with a nasty and arousing doctor, and a hell of an examination as the centerpiece. A shutterbug couple's ritual of going to a strange pagoda in their neighborhood and having secretive full-moon sex takes a turn in Sommer Marsden's "Pagoda" when he ups the ante by blindfolding her and making the encounter more public than private. Donna George Storey's "A Wider World" reveals what happens when two couples try having slow, at first fairly tame sex in front of each other; until our heroine can't take the tease and jumps right into a beautiful ménage with her husband.

You can feel the furious arousal when the fighting couple in "All's Fair," by Tiffani Angus, escalate their confrontation as she strips off to take a bath and he chases after her, only to get a lesson in being a gracious loser in a searingly surprising sexual encounter. Dorianne's "Neighborly Relations" is what happens when a girl has boring sex with a guy who brags to his friends about it—only to have her say *Oh no you didn't* and throw down the gauntlet for him to make her come, culminating in a surprise development where everyone's invited to play. The tension of conflicted desire becomes lushly heated in "Let Me In," by The Empress, in which a young Indian woman fights with her sometime lover, a hot, uncouth guy, climaxing in a white-knuckle ride of a sexual scenario.

Languid and lyrical, "Lolita," by Zahara Stardust, follows a young, free-spirited female backpacker into exotic locales, notably one where she meets a very handsome and sexy older man and invites us into their sexual exchanges full of playful flirtation and hot sex.

Lip-licking delicious is how I'll describe "The Gourmet," by Chaparrita. In it, a female restaurant owner and chef, famous in the United States and on vacation in Mexico, has three different smutty and taste-inspired encounters with local men, from whom she gets just what she wants. Valerie Alexander's "The Magicians" begins at a reunion of old friends where a woman sees again for the first time since graduation her one-time boyfriend and his best friend, with whom she had a failed threeway. This time, she's surprised when the guys are hot for her and each other, and the unexpected results will have you hot for the possibilities found in the power of three.

I hope you find these stories as unforgettable, surprising and erotically inspiring as I do. These writers are stars, and my only caution for you going forward from this page is to expect the unexpected.

Violet Blue
San Francisco

DROUGHT

Olivia Glass

Halfway down the highway, she is imagining his hand inside of her.

The image displaces all of her musings about the goats grazing on the hill she just passed and whether she's paid her electric bill. She swerves slightly, her wheels flirting with the double yellow line. Another motorist honks, and she brings herself back in time to avoid an accident.

Deep inside of her, something twinges; her mind thrumming across a cello string that runs from belly button to clitoris, notes resonating up her spine. Her mouth parts a little, an *oh* rising to her lips; her hands tighten around the wheel.

A ripple of illuminated brake lights starts near the tunnel entrance and surges back toward her. Cars slow and then stop. She presses the ball of her bare foot into the brake pedal, breathing out with the motion, and rolls down her window, straining to see what's happened.

Ah. A fender bender near the entrance of the tunnel. The

drivers climb out of their cars. She can almost hear the groans of the other motorists, rising up like heavy smog that hangs above their vehicle roofs.

"Fuck me," she intones. She turns on the radio, but the stream of breathless news is too much for a day like this. A flick of her wrist, and the speakers go silent.

The heat that rises from the blacktop begins to seep into her car. She lifts a leg from beneath her skirt and rests it against the dashboard. Her eyes glance at the car next to her, where the driver is slowly drumming his fingers on the top of the steering wheel, his other hand out of sight.

What if he's jerking—

The thought is only half formed, and she feels a burning sensation rising in her face. It isn't so much a blush—she doesn't blush, not anymore—but a flush of heat that comes from somewhere deep inside her, prickling on her skin. There's another twinge between her legs.

She bites her lip, harder than she intends. Her tongue probes the cut and she tastes copper. Her mind begins to wander away from the car, back to her house; back to the four-poster bed that she had to leave this morning, a man beneath the red sheets, a suit crumpled on the hardwood floor.

That suit. It feels like he's always emerged from the day in a starched shirt and tie, dress pants, belted, and those shiny shoes in which she can see her own reflection. She loves the way he comes through the door—loosening his tie, tugging the knot down, letting the fabric slide out of his collar. There is so much promise in that motion. She loves the way the tie slides.

Someone honks. At the tunnel entrance, there is no sign of movement.

Her fingers are roaming over her damp underwear.

She glances at the shoulder of the road: only a few feet of

space before the road narrows and there is nowhere to go. Does she have enough room? The car purrs as she yanks her wheel to the right and pulls off.

Domino effect: the lane where she had been sitting shifts exactly one car length. Drivers look up; hope flashes across their faces. When they realize that the traffic is still stopped, they rest back in their seats, annoyed.

She, however, is free.

Slipping on her flip-flops, she pushes open the door and steps onto the road. The pavement is sticky from the heat, and her soles cling to the blacktop with every step. A few people watch her, confused. She looks up at the hill. Parts of it are bare and exposed to the sun, but there are whole swaths covered in trees.

She begins to climb.

The hill is steep, but not too steep. Her sandals don't last long. As she scrambles over some rocks, one slips from her foot and falls away. The other, then, is useless; she takes it off and places it in the crevice between two rocks. Her car grows smaller, the traffic becoming less real and more like meticulously arranged toy cars with every minute.

The grass is hot and dry and crunches beneath her feet. God! California. She marvels at the images that she'd always harbored of a California dense with lush, green summer vegetation, and how wrong they were. This grass is brown, and it hasn't rained in months. No wonder everything is dying. It isn't like this in Pennsylvania. There, hot summer days are punctuated by violent thunderstorms; lightning slicing open the sky, thunder making the windowpanes rattle, rain turning the streets into narrow rivers where the water writhes and gushes. There is something so satisfying about those storms, about the release after the day's long and agonizing heat. But California—no. The summer is just one big denial.

She reaches a shady alcove, sits beneath a tree, and leans her back against the thick, knotty bark.

The belt always follows the tie. Oh fuck, the belt. She loves the metallic click as he unbuckles it, the *shhhh* as he slides it from its loops. The belt means business. She lies in the bed watching this—the tie, the belt, *shhhh*—her hand buried between her legs, fingers sliding through her wet topography. And then the pants drop, easily.

In the white starched shirt and white briefs, he stands next to her. She always wears a soft black housedress when he comes over—no bra, no underwear. He stands there peering down at her, her hand moving steadily beneath the blanket, her nipples hard points beneath the thin cotton. And he smiles. He always smiles.

The traffic is out of sight. The highway is visible, but only as a thin, meandering line, silver in the sun. She can see the white steel skeletons on the edge of Oakland, the glittering bay, the hilly urban landscape of San Francisco and the wide expanse of ocean.

She licks her lip; it stings. She looks up.

She can go higher.

She continues ascending. The grass changes. Some of it rises higher than the rest, tickling her skin. She reaches down and runs her hands along the blades' feathery tips. The trees open up into a large field, and she charges through it, grabbing fistfuls of grass and wildflowers and ripping them up by their roots with a savagery that thrills her. She swings in a circle and lets the flora go flying. A wanton scream tears from her lungs, careening across the field like a flash flood. Birds rise, startled. She laughs, her throat raw, her chest heaving.

She keeps moving.

He is always hard when he kicks the pants away. She can

see his cock, angled against his torso, held there by the fabric of his underwear. If she is in a teasing mood, she'll lift a free finger and trace it along the firm length, making him shiver. Sometimes she'll work that finger through the slit of the fly, touching the silky-smooth skin. But if she's feeling ravenous she'll sit up in the bed, tugging down the elastic band, and catch his cock in her mouth as it springs free.

All of the men she's ever been with before have been silent, even when they came. But not him. No, the warmth of her mouth around him evokes a beautiful moan, ragged as if it were being dragged across stones. She releases him from her mouth long enough to pull the tip of her tongue along his cock. When her tongue catches the ridge beneath the head, a drop of precome beads, and she catches it with her lips, salty. He comes down and kisses her, hard. She tells him how wet she is.

She feels as if the physics of her body are changing, here on the hill, as if the air is getting thinner, though that can't be—she isn't that high up. Her heart pounds harder, and each beat seems sluggish but thunderously loud. She can feel her blood's movement in her fingers, her heartbeat in her cunt.

He cannot wait. He shoves the black dress up past her hips and consumes her, messily, as if he is devouring a piece of fruit. He writhes against the bed, sucking slowly, steadily on her clit. And then—oh, Jesus, here she has to stop moving—and then he brings up fingers to go inside of her. When they'd begun, he'd hesitantly used one, maybe two, but now he starts with three and goes up, because he knows. He understands what she wants. By now, she is so wet and open that once he hits four she asks for another, and he holds his thumb close to his palm, working it around inside of her. The walls of her cunt pull at his hand, perfect in its size, and as he twists his hand and sucks on her— fuck, fuck—she comes in waves, the muscles around his hands convulsing like a truck braking over miles and miles of road.

As she begins to reenter her body, he gently slips his hand out of her—she releases him with a shudder of pleasure—and comes up to her face, kissing her neck and the corner of her mouth.

She reaches another patch of trees and picks her way along the knotted roots and cool shadows. He continues to flit across her mind. The belt. Silk and cotton. Mouth, hands. Miles and miles.

The trees end, and for a dizzying second, she can see nothing but sky.

The whole valley comes into focus. The cities glimmer slightly, insignificant, but the distant hills glow gold in the light of the sinking sun. The ridges are purple and hazy with distance, puckered and raised like a spine. She lifts her hand and imagines her fingers running over the range, dipping into the pockets of the canyons and lowlands, rising up with the swell of the knolls. Mountains. Are they mountains? She's lost all sense of perception. The sea and the bay and the rush of the city are at her back, the open expanse of Californian wilderness lies before her. *Fuck*. It isn't quite a thought and it isn't quite a sound. The word comes out as a breath, as awe.

She breathes deeply and lies down on the grass.

The blades prick through the thin fabric of her shirt. The breeze whispers to her, across her. She slides her skirt up her legs and settles it around her hips. The wind teases her, gently. Her left hand drifts across her breasts, slowly stroking her erect nipple.

She has never been so awake or alive; her nerves are naked wires, her skin the wet pavement during a lightning storm. Her mind frees itself, expands. She feels as if a fault line along her breastbone has come apart, and now she is open to the air, her lungs expanding like slick balloons into the dusty ozone, her heart throbbing.

She watches him, soaking wet but not finished. He rolls the condom on and squares himself between her thighs. The sensation of this is almost too much, and she gasps as he moves into her. He moans and loses control of his words, which flow out of him like warm, uncorked champagne. "Fuck—god, you feel—fuck, you're so—god, god—fuck—" She reaches up, tangles her fingers in his hair and pulls him down to her neck. He speaks the words into her skin.

The valley is ablaze with color, with light. She hears nothing but her own ragged breathing. She closes her eyes. She touches herself—dripping, swollen. She lets out a slow, throaty moan, her fingers stroking her clit over and over again.

Him, asleep beneath the sheets. Him, wrist deep inside her, bent over her body and slick with sweat. His teeth on her throat, her nails in his back. His weight pinning her down to the mattress. Him biting his lip in pleasure. The want surges through her, mingling with the yes and now and carrying light to the very tips of her fingers and soles of her feet. Sweat glistens on her arms, pooling behind her knees, in the crooks of her elbows.

Her back begins to arch. Her hand leaves her breast and digs into the ground, pulling chunks of dirt as easily as she grabs handfuls of soft cotton sheets. The earth is breathing, writhing beneath its skin. Her right hand draws hard circles over, and over, and over, and she feels the climax surging toward her, tumbling into her gravity.

The orgasm fills her, powerful and steady. She knows she cannot drown. Instead, she overflows.

The sky is darkening—purple and navy and preparing for bed. Insects thrum their legs together from the trees.

He always collapses on her, breathing heavily. She holds him and whispers in his ear, "Come down, come down, come back to me." They stay there for a long time, tangled, wet and quiet.

She lies in the grass and laughs. She laughs and laughs, and her face is wet with tears. She doesn't remember crying.

Sleep comes swiftly.

She will only wake up to the *tap tap tap* of a gentle, predawn rain on her cheeks, spotting her shirt and running into her mouth in gentle rivulets. She will climb down the mountain. Eventually.

And she will return home, where he waits for her on the damp porch.

TWEETUP

Louise Lush

I sipped my wine and surveyed the swish hotel bar with growing apprehension. *Should have stayed at home*, I thought. *This was a stupid idea.*

I didn't recognize a single face amid the small throng of people, although they all seemed to know each other. I knew them too, of course, but only online and only via their various anonymous handles and avatars.

The concept of a Twitter meetup had seemed appealing when it was first suggested by a friend with a large following. It was an opportunity to put names to faces, to have a few drinks and to discuss issues in more than just 140 characters. In the face of my increasingly closeted online life, it seemed like a good chance to get out of the house and socialize, in the old-fashioned way.

Now, however, I regretted my bold foray into the meatworld. Here I had to worry about how I looked and what I said. And I had to remember the social graces, which included the imponderable problem of what to do when everyone else is engaged in conversation and you're standing there, unknown and ignored.

I took a swig of my wine and tried to think of a way to introduce myself. *Hi, I'm QueenAngie. I'm the one who always tweets about my pet frogs and the porn I've been watching.*

Somehow, it just didn't seem right.

I felt a tap on my shoulder and turned to face a tall, intelligent-looking man with a square jaw and small, round-rimmed glasses. He was in his midthirties, dressed casually in jeans and a T-shirt that said TWITTER=OBSESSION. He was smiling at me kindly and holding out his hand.

"Hi, nice to meet you. I only just got here; thought I'd introduce myself. I'm Scott, although on Twitter I'm Geekguy77."

My startled, slightly panicked expression changed to a smile of recognition as I returned his handshake. "Oh, *you*. The IT guy with the Apple jokes. You should write for the newspapers!"

He grinned at my compliment. "And you are?"

My smile slipped a little and I felt my stomach turn over. Did I really want to reveal my dirty, true online self to real-world people like this?

But it was too late. I was here, I'd committed to this. And these were my Internet friends, after all. They were *different*.

"I'm…er…I'm Angie. QueenAngie."

He raised his eyebrows just a little, his smile becoming lopsided. "Ahhh. You." I felt myself blushing. "Yes, I follow you. How are the frogs?"

I laughed, perhaps a little too loudly. "They're fine. Although I can't get Arthur out of his castle at the moment."

"Sounds like a case of Frog Depression to me. Hey, can I get you another wine?"

I considered my near-empty glass and nodded. "What the hell, a bit more social lubricant never hurt anyone. Thanks." He smiled and headed toward the bar. I watched him as he went, finding myself admiring his physique. *This guy might be in IT, but he obviously takes care of himself,* I thought. Look at that butt.

My gaze wandered. The crowd hadn't grown in the last few moments but it did feel a lot less threatening. Amazing what one friendly face can do.

Scott returned holding a beer and a glass of wine. I could see him studying me as he approached. I wondered if my appearance matched his idea of my online persona. I suspected it didn't. In real life I'm fairly average looking, although I do think I have agreeable brown eyes and I try to stay fit.

"I should have recognized you," Scott said as he handed me my glass.

"How?"

"Your hoop earrings. You wrote you always wore them. A few weeks ago?

I thought for a moment. "That's right, I did. Gee, you pay attention."

He smiled. "I like your tweets."

I laughed. "Now there's a twenty-first-century compliment."

We fell into a very easy conversation, comparing thoughts on politics, computers and whether Stephen Fry was worth following anymore. Scott seemed to hang on every word I said, eager to hear my opinion, his eyes always on me, seemingly oblivious to the rest of the room. I felt flattered by his attention and found myself responding in kind, drawn to his presence, keen to hear what he had to say. The wine had started to kick in and I felt warm and happy in his company. I also felt more than a little flirtatious.

"Are you married, Geekguy?" I asked.

"Uh, no, not yet," he said. "IT guy, remember? That means lots of lonely nights at home eating two-minute noodles and playing *World of Warcraft.*"

I nodded, laughing at the stereotype. "Yeah, me too. Just me and the frogs."

"And the porn."

I shrugged, blushing. "Uh, yeah, the porn."

"I like how you tweet about porn."

"Really?" I gave him a shy smile. "It's just for fun."

"I like the jokes, but you do make a lot of perceptive points." I realized he was regarding me intently.

"I probably shouldn't be so open about watching porn. I figured it would put people off here."

He shook his head. "No, not at all. Not me, anyway. It means you're interesting, not inhibited." He gave me a long look. "It's sexy."

I blushed again. "Thank you." I didn't know what else to say.

"To be honest, I've often wondered about you," he said.

"You have?"

He took a sip of his drink. "Yes. I wondered what you were like in real life. If you were anything like the woman I imagined QueenAngie to be."

My heart began to beat a little faster and I felt a little flustered, knowing we were getting into dangerous territory. Still, the wine egged me on. "And what is it you imagine?"

"Well, some days I wonder if you're sitting there tweeting wearing suspenders and a lacy bra."

"Ha!" I chuckled. "Track pants more like."

He smiled and nodded. "Other days I think you might be like one of those pulp fiction librarians, all prim and proper on the outside but really dirty once you get past the façade."

"Well, I just have an office job. Kinda boring, I'm afraid."

He smiled again, but then he leaned his face in closer to me and lowered his voice. "And some days I think of you as the perfect partner. Uninhibited and eager. A woman who loves sex, who knows what she wants in bed and knows how to get it."

My throat had gone dry. "That... I could be like that, I guess."

He moved in even closer and whispered in my ear. "I think you are like that. Because some days I think of you as my lover. Some days I imagine you fucking me."

He drew back and looked at me, his eyes full of desire. I couldn't breathe and I could barely think. My heart thudded with amazement at what he'd just said.

And meanwhile, my cunt clenched in response.

Eventually he said, "I'm staying at this hotel."

I held his gaze for a few more moments, blushing. And then I gave him the smallest nod. I don't know why I did it, but at that moment, it felt right.

We didn't look at each other as we walked out of the bar and toward the elevators. There was something absurd about the whole situation but at that moment I didn't care. All I could think about was the sensation of absolute desire that had overwhelmed me, the instinctual emotional and physical need that emanated from my heart and from my cunt.

This man, this stranger, wanted to fuck me and I couldn't wait to return the favor.

The doors opened on an empty elevator and we casually walked in. Scott pressed the button for floor twelve. It seemed to take forever for the doors to glide shut but the moment they closed he was kissing me, his hands cupping my cheeks, his lips surprisingly soft. He tasted of beer and lust and I felt his cock pressing against me through his jeans, eager and urgent.

The elevator dinged and the doors opened on floor eight. We quickly pulled apart as another hotel guest entered. I was flushed and felt embarrassed but Scott kept hold of my hand as the doors closed. We rode the rest of the way in silence and then he led me out of the elevator and down the hall, stopping at the door of his room.

He studied me briefly. "Are you sure you want to do this?" he asked, concern mingling with the heat in his eyes. I only nodded, my heart pounding with excitement.

The second the door closed we were kissing again, harder and stronger this time. His hands were in my hair and I could smell his masculine scent, a mix of aftershave and lusty sweat. He greedily unbuttoned my shirt and pushed down my bra, his tongue laving across my now-erect nipple. It gave me goose bumps and further awakened the hungry beast of desire that was uncoiling inside me.

He pushed me back on the soft hotel bed, unzipped and pulled down my jeans and panties, spreading my legs open before dipping his head between my thighs. He licked me with a determined desperation and I responded in kind, moaning and pushing his head into my crotch, skewing his glasses sideways across his face.

He had imagined me as a wanton, uninhibited sexual goddess. I decided to live up to his fantasy.

Not that I had to try hard. Every nerve in my body thrummed with desire. My pussy was hot and wet and open for him, throbbing with blood and attuned to every nuance of pleasure. I felt like I could come then and there, without even trying.

Indeed, I almost did, except that Scott paused and stripped off his own clothing. I lay back, panting, and admired his well-proportioned body with its nicely defined muscles and hairy chest. His cock jutted in front of him like a salute as he rolled on a condom. It curved slightly upward and was delightfully thick. The last thing he removed was his glasses.

"Come on then," I said with smoldering eyes. "Fuck me like you imagined fucking me."

He practically threw himself on me, his mouth covering mine, his cock sliding easily into my moist cunt. I wrapped my legs around him as he plunged into me, a long groan of pent-up satisfaction escaping him. I wanted to hold him close, to feel his flesh against mine as he fucked me, to connect with him completely.

Yet after a minute he sat back, pulling out of me. "No," he said. "I want you on top."

I obliged, straddling him and impaling myself on that lovely thick cock. He kept his eyes on me the whole time, watching my body and my face as the sensations flowed through me.

"How's this?" I asked. "Is this what you wanted?"

He nodded and licked his lips. I kissed him then, slowly and passionately, enjoying the feel of his mouth against mine, softness against softness. Part of me felt amazed that he even wanted me, plain old Angie who worked in an office. And yet at that moment I felt exalted by his desire for me.

And then I began to fuck him hard and fast, reaching down to rub my clit as I moved. His hands moved to my breasts, caressing my nipples as I rode him with my head tossed back. I was Queen-Angie, the sex queen, the slut and the goddess in one, the ultimate woman and the perfect partner. I imagined myself as her and, as the pleasure mounted, I became her. Nothing else mattered but this moment and this man, my body a conduit for glory.

I was already so close, my orgasm didn't take long to arrive. As if hit by a shower of stars, I was blinded by pure ecstasy, moaning and shuddering with joy, gushing onto his cock.

"God, you're beautiful," he said.

It was almost too much and I collapsed forward onto him in the aftermath, gasping.

He continued to fuck me as I nestled against him. Within moments, he came, groaning into my ear. I quickly rose and looked at his face, suffused with so much pleasure. He was utterly vulnerable at that moment, like a lost soul, his handsome face devoid of anything except intense physical delight.

I realized I wanted to see that again.

I stayed astride him as the spasms subsided, watching him. Eventually he opened his eyes.

"Thank you," he said.

I smiled and stroked his cheek. "I don't often come that easily. I should be thanking you."

"You were exactly how I imagined."

I grinned sardonically. "Well, I have a reputation to live up to. QueenAngie, the Twitter Sex Goddess." I rolled off and snuggled up to him. "Now, if only I had a phone."

"Why?"

"Gotta tweet my latest review."

He looked startled. "You wouldn't—?"

I let it hang for a moment, then laughed. "No. Of course I wouldn't. Why would I want to share this with anyone else? It's too perfect. Besides, you can't put a fuck that good into one hundred and forty characters."

He grinned and pulled me closer. "Maybe I should tell the world about you. 'Geekguy finds woman of his dreams at Tweetup.'"

I raised my eyebrows. "But we've only just met."

He shook his head. "No, we haven't. I know you. I've known you for months online. You're there, being you in everything you write. You're smart, you're funny, you're kind...I've admired you for so long. We just have to get to know each other in a physical sense."

"Well, we've already made a helluva good start."

He laughed and rolled out of bed. "Come on. I'm taking you out to dinner. That's what normal people do, you know. And maybe tomorrow you can introduce me to the frogs."

I laughed and got dressed. And then we went on our first date.

After dinner, I couldn't help myself. I picked up the phone and added a new update to my Twitter profile.

Met @geekguy77 at the Tweetup. Nice guy. Says he can cure frog depression. We'll see.

EDDIE'S ALL-NIGHT DINER

K. D. Grace

I watch a man in a pin-striped suit feed his dressed-for-success colleague lemon meringue pie. What starts as the old I'll-let-you-taste-mine-if-you-let-me-taste-yours ploy rapidly evolves into oral sex on a fork, tongues darting, lips smacking and teeth just barely grazing the flash of stainless steel as they devour sweet tart creaminess. A generous dollop of meringue topples slo-mo off his fork down into his colleague's generous cleavage. They both laugh nervously, and she doesn't decline his help with extricating the offending egg whites. She opens the top button of her blouse and thrusts push-up bra tits against his proffered napkin. It's clear to me they'd both much prefer he use his tongue.

The place is particularly crowded, and no one notices me squirming in the corner booth, with my imagination fanning the flames, inventing numerous scenarios to fit the covert business meeting that brings this pair to Eddie's All-Night Diner after hours. Their briefcases are still in tow; their BlackBerries are perched on the table at the ready. But they're sitting side by side instead of across from each other. Clearly the unprofessional invasion of personal space doesn't concern them. But it very much concerns me. Amazing how slick Naugahyde gets beneath an excited bare cunt.

Once the cleavage is de-meringued and the pie is eaten, Mr. and Ms. Fortune 500 don't linger long enough to actually get me off. But I've seen enough to start my pussy buzzing at a low, moist thrum. I'm not exactly horned out, but I'm definitely feeling the love.

As one might deduce from the name, Eddie's All-Night Diner isn't listed in the *Michelin Guide*. That's fine by me. I'll be the first to admit I'm a philistine where food is concerned. I don't think so much about how food tastes as I do about how food is eaten and the context in which it's enjoyed—or not.

Eddie's is all about context. Interesting people come to Eddie's after everything else in the city closes up for the night, and they bring their interesting contexts along with them. Add that to the fact that people tend to be a little off their guard in the wee hours, and let the entertainment begin!

You can learn a lot about a person by watching him eat—if you're discreet, that is. People get uncomfortable when someone ogles them while they shovel in their eggs, or sculpt their mashed potatoes with a spoon or cut up their spaghetti Bolognese with a fork. But I have great peripheral vision, which makes me an expert at discretion.

All the waitresses know I'm a night owl and that I tip well, so they're happy to leave me to it when I show up with some random magazine or a novel that I know full well I'll only pretend to read because nothing in a magazine or a novel can compare to the entertainment on Eddie's menu.

I always arrive a little before ten, just before the theaters and cinemas let out. The club crowd comes later, but I have no place else to be, so I can wait. Tonight's special is ribs, but I order a toasted cheese sandwich, something I can eat with one hand, something that won't distract me.

I watch the wilted couples pour in off the steamy summer street. I listen as they heave collective sighs of relief at that first breath of the air conditioner against the sweaty backs of their necks. Those people who share menus, I watch with special interest. They're more likely to wrap themselves around each other, using the experience of choosing food as an opportunity to grope. They're more likely to feed each other ice cream and Banoffee pie and playfully snatch fries and prawns from each others' plate. They're also more likely to partake of dessert not offered on the menu.

In the booth to my left I take in the peripheral show as a young redhead wraps darkly painted lips around a straw and draws up a slow, thick mouthful of vanilla shake with a prolonged slurp. Her date's wearing an oversized Oregon State T-shirt in an effort to look bulkier, but it just makes him look sloppy. He shifts in his seat, his eyes locked on hers. But I'm betting his peripheral vision is at least as good as mine. I'm betting he's actually admiring the way the tops of her tits peek from under her plunging neckline all ripe, round fruit-like. I'm betting he's hoping her nipples will actually succeed in their magnificent attempt to drill through her blouse in the heavy air-conditioning. I'm betting he's thinking how much more tasty they'd be than the cheeseburger and the fries he's drowned under half a bottle of catsup.

I drop my napkin on the floor and duck beneath the table for a peek. As I suspected, his hand is shifting almost imperceptibly against the swelling front of his jeans, assurance that I'm right about his peripheral vision. Above deck he's stuffing fries and burger in his mouth in a feeding frenzy. No doubt he'll need lots of energy if he gets what he's hoping for. She's nibbling her fries all dainty-like, licking the dribbles of catsup from the underside with delicate pink flicks of her tongue. I wonder if the grand finale will be at his house or hers, or maybe they live in the dorms, and their fellow students will hear them grunting and thrusting through the thin walls and maybe enjoy a bit of secondary sex while they listen.

I shift in my seat and feel the grab of vinyl against bare skin. I always wear a short flip skirt and no panties when I visit Eddie's. That's my uniform. I pride myself on being an expert at stealth orgasms. My technique is more efficient without panties. I don't usually wear a bra either. My tits aren't big, but they're not small, and they're quite heavy. When I'm braless, I notice just how heavy they are, how they tug and pull at my chest like they're demanding my full attention, like they won't give up until they get it. But I always wear something loose. After all, I don't go to Eddie's to draw attention to myself.

I've long since finished my toasted cheese. On an impulse, I order the raspberry crème brûlée from the waitress and turn my attention back to the redhead and her burgeoning boyfriend.

He looks like he's about to burst. His hand is now press-press-pressing against his bulge. I don't have to look under the table again to know. I can see the subtle but rhythmic tensing of the muscles of his forearms and the way he holds his back stiff, letting his fingers do the walking. Oh, he's found the sweet spot, all right. My pussy quivers. Maybe he can't wait. Maybe he'll shove that sassy little miniskirt up over Red's pert round bottom right here in the alley behind Eddie's. Maybe he'll twiddle the fat lips of her pussy until she's open and wet and begging for it. Maybe with her braced against the wall, he'll shove right in, give her a good, hard jack hammering and take a load off.

"May I share your table?"

I jump at the unexpected intrusion and jerk my guilty peripherals away from the couple.

"Sorry, I didn't mean to startle you, are you all right?" The voice is a resonant baritone that I could easily curl up and purr in.

"Fine," I say, and I find myself looking up, and up, and up at a mountain of a man. Not fat, mind you—far from it. He's well proportioned and displayed in a muscle shirt stretched over—well—big muscles, tight muscles, muscles that set everything beneath my skirt aquiver. He carries a rolled-up newspaper tucked under his arm. He wears loose-fitting summer shorts that come just to his knees and a pair of Birkenstocks the size of small cruise ships. I have never seen feet so big. I know it's cliché, but I can't help wondering just how well proportioned he really is. I nod to the other side of my booth and offer a polite smile. There are other tables available. But it doesn't matter. I'm intrigued by the size of his Birkenstocks.

His long legs jostle mine as he sits down, offering an embarrassed apology. My stomach does a pirouette. The brush of flesh against flesh is something I'm quite familiar with here at Eddie's, but I've never actually felt it myself. I pretend to find my place in the copy of *Anna Karenina* I've been bringing with me for the past month, then I pretend to lose myself in the story. He opens the menu flat on the table and leans over it, one thick finger following down the list of entrées. He's leaned over the table so far that he's practically engulfing it. Just a little sniff and I catch the scent of high summer and man-heat in his hair, and I feel ripples low in my belly.

"What'll you have?"

I start at the sound of the waitress's bored voice.

"I'll have the ribs," he says.

The combined stares of my table companion and the waitress are my clue that the little whimper I thought was only mental has actually made its way past my lips and out into the public domain.

"Sorry," I say nodding down to the open pages of my novel. "Very moving."

He gives me a look that might be sympathetic. The waitress only shoves her pad in her apron and strides back to the counter with the man's order—the order for ribs.

Nothing is more revealing about a person than the way he eats ribs. I would never touch them. I'd just feel too vulnerable. The man with the huge Birkenstocks is going to sit right here in front of the queen of food intuition and expose himself.

I can't believe my luck.

But then it hits me. I'm not watching him safely from a corner somewhere. How stealthy can I be when the man is practically sitting on my lap?

He pushes aside the menu, opens his paper flat on the table and starts to read like it's no big deal.

There are tables full of people all around us. They're all eating and drinking and exposing themselves to me, but suddenly all I notice is the man sitting across from me, occasionally brushing my knee with his.

My crème brûlée arrives and I stare down at it, suddenly too timid to crack the burnt sugar shell and wriggle my spoon down through the smooth creaminess to the tart, plump raspberries at the bottom.

"Looks good," he says, smiling up at me.

Just then his ribs arrive—a mountain of ribs, slathered in rich, savory barbeque sauce, steam rising in little swirls like a bevy of miniature dancing girls wafting their way upward. The waitress slaps down a couple of extra napkins and a plate for the bones and leaves us to it.

When she's gone I force a smile. "Those look good too." My

voice sounds breathless and thin, like it's gone off to chase after the rib-scented dancing girls.

"I love ribs," he says. "I love food I can eat with my fingers, food it's all right to be messy with."

I barely manage to suppress another whimper, and my pussy suddenly feels as sticky as the ribs.

"*Bon appétit*," he says, nodding to my crème brûlée.

"*Bon appétit*," I manage to rasp.

He lifts the biggest, thickest, most succulent rib to his lips, one sopping with barbeque sauce and dripping with juice. Then he bites into the steamy meaty side of it, his gaze never leaving mine. I give the burnt sugar shell of my crème brûlée a sharp rap with my spoon, unable to take my eyes of the catlike way his tongue snakes up the bone, the way his teeth peel back the meat, the way the juice drips down his fingers and his chin, all so unselfconsciously done, all so deliciously carnivorous. A meat-eater through and through, a primal force to be reckoned with: my god, he's magnificent!

As he tosses the spent bone onto the extra plate and lifts a second rib to his lips, I mirror his actions with my first spoonful of crème brûlée, rich and velvety with just the tip of a single raspberry peaking out from under the crème like a tart, pink nipple. He laps the droplets of meat juice and sauce from the end of the rib just before it can drip onto the table, catching the dribble that slides down his chin on the end of his finger, which he shoves into his mouth, licking and sucking all the way to his knuckle.

I gasp, and he raises a questioning eyebrow.

"Good. It's good," I force my breathless voice around a creamy mouthful.

He nods his agreement with a juicy smile and a flutter of dark lashes.

I eat my dessert in big, lusty bites, swallowing down the texture of cream and the tang of raspberry overlaid by the bite of burnt sugar. He's like a lion at the kill. I half expect him to snarl as he rips the meat from the bone. Just when I'm beginning to suspect that for him, the pleasure of meat is a total body experience, I realize he's watching me watch him eat. He's watching me rock and shift against the Naugahyde seat with the ecstatic pleasure of the overall experience.

I freeze. A flash of heat rises to my face like the air conditioner is suddenly blowing hot air. Carefully, I lay down my spoon and wipe the corners of my mouth demurely.

He offers a lazy smile, tosses aside another bone and wipes his mouth, before lowering the napkin back into his lap. "You enjoy food, don't you?"

I blush harder. "I might say the same about you."

His smile expands to a soft chuckle. "You can learn so much about people by watching them eat. Don't you agree?"

My stomach somersaults. Has he read my mind? I've always thought watching people eat was almost like reading their minds, but I thought that was my little secret. And granted the choice of the crème brûlée was a bit flashy on my part, but I never imagined someone would actually watch me eat.

His knee, which has been resting lightly against the outside of mine, shifts and maneuvers until it's positioned between my legs, and I catch my breath with the delicious impropriety of it. But he just continues eating like it's no big deal. He's gnawing and slurping and licking and all the while his knee is gently rubbing against the inside of mine.

I'm in the middle of a luscious creamy mouthful when I feel his leg withdraw. Then he shifts slightly in the booth without missing a beat in his efficient devouring of ribs, and before I know it, his knee has been replaced by his warm, bare foot. It snakes its way up the inside of my thigh, pushing and scrunching my skirt ahead of it as it goes. He seems to be completely focused on his ribs, nipping and ripping and making yummy little animal sounds, almost as though he's completely unaware of what his very naughty foot is doing under the table.

I'm a captive audience. And after all this time, all my observations and fantasies at Eddie's All-Night Diner come home to roost, right between my legs. Under the table I rearrange my skirt and shift my bottom, opening my legs a little wider until I'm sure the approach is clear, all the while eating crème brûlée like nobody's business.

He makes circular motions high on the inside of my thigh with long, expressive toes. I'm glad the noisy clatter of dishes and the babble of a full house cover my involuntary gasps and sighs. Here I am acting like one of them, one of those people I quietly and smugly observe night in, night out. But I forget all about that when the ball of his foot presses against my mons, caressing my tightly trimmed curls, gently tap-tap-tapping against my pubic bone. And all the while he's chomping and gnawing like king carnivore himself come to feast.

I run my tongue over the bottom of the spoon, slurping back a mouthful of brûlée goodness, and I imagine doing the same to his cock. I wonder just how much of it I could fit into my mouth. Surely he must be hard and uncomfortable. Surely he must be aching for some relief. He shifts against the booth and grunts softly, almost as though he's read my thoughts again. Then his big toe dips to circle my clit, and I practically bounce off the seat, barely managing to collect myself as the waitress comes by to refill our water glasses. A little more maneuvering and he's tweaking me between his big toe and the second toe. It's almost like he's got a third set of fingers under the table fiddling between my legs like they know their way around the place.

I can't reach his cock. My legs aren't long enough. I'll have to rely on visual stimulation. With the hand not shoveling dessert into my mouth, I reach up under my blouse and play with my tits. They feel so stretched and heavy, like they're trying to get to him. I pinch my nipples until they're as big as the raspberries in my crème brûlée, and he watches like he has X-ray vision. The toe dance intensifies and his Schwarzenegger pecs rise and fall as though eating ribs has suddenly become hard labor.

I shamelessly undo the front of my blouse, watching his eyes get bigger and bigger with each button. And when the waitress's back is turned and I'm pretty sure no one's looking, I let the blouse gape open. I knead and cup and pinch until I can see his pulse hammering against his temples, and his chest is heaving so hard I fear he'll rip the seams out of the muscle shirt like he's the Incredible Hulk.

He shifts and maneuvers, and with a tight, sharp thrust, suddenly his big toe pushes into my grudging pussy, and goddamned if it isn't almost as big as the average cock! Or at least that's how if feels all thrust up inside me.

"Messy business, ribs," I rasp. My pussy clenches tight around his toe and I wince as he slips in a second. "So juicy." I force the words between gritted teeth.

"I told you, I like messy food." He finds his rhythm. It's a subtle rhythm, a rhythm no one else notices, though I'd like to think I would have noticed if it had been happening to someone else. The tight rocking and straining of his hips convinces me that I may not be the only one skilled in the art of stealth orgasms. With amazing finesse, he eases yet another toe into my dilating pout, and I'm suddenly so full, I feel like I'll split in two. But I just keep pressing harder and harder onto him because I can't help myself, because I've never been foot-fucked before and because he's just so damned, deliciously huge! I can feel the connection between our bodies, I can feel the shifting of his weight from one buttock to the other and I can almost hear the slurping of my wet cunt grasping at his toes, hungrily sucking in every bit of him until there's absolutely no room for more.

He stops eating ribs. I stop eating crème brulee. His face is red, and I'm sure mine is too. I'm grinding against him like I'm riding a big horse and his muscles go so tight I fear he'll strain something, and god what I wouldn't give for a peek under the table.

The tightly swallowed yelp is mine as my pussy convulses and I feel the orgasm exploding all the way up through the crown of my head. The groan wrapped in baritone silk is his. His face scrunches briefly, and he inhales sharply like he's in pain, then I feel something warm and sticky against my knee and the top of my bare thigh.

We both sit stunned as the waitress approaches to refill our coffee cups. "I think I'll need a few more napkins," he says sweetly to the woman. He doesn't sound at all like someone who's just shot his load under the table on the bare thigh of a stranger in an all-night diner.

From her apron pocket, the waitress hurriedly slaps down enough napkins to paper the walls of the ladies room and trots off to wait on a party of eight two tables down.

When he's sure she's gone, he takes several napkins from the stack and proceeds to wipe his cock like it's no big deal. The man is actually wiping his cock under the table with half his foot still buried in my cunt. The very thought makes my pussy grasp and twitch again. Considerately he waits until I stop spasming before slowly, one at a time, he slips his toes out from between my pussy lips and offers a little nod of his head to the stack of napkins.

Blushing clear to the roots of my hair, I grab a handful and do my own stealth cleanup beneath the table, while he smiles down at me like I'm a well-behaved child.

The waitress clears the dishes and brings his check. I go back to pretending to read *Anna Karenina*. Once he's paid, he grabs his newspaper and stands to go. But as he does so, he moves to my side of the booth, and I strain my neck to look up at him. "Thanks for sharing your table," he says. Then he leans down to meet my gaze. "I hear next Friday night is surf and turf. The steak's a little overcooked for my taste, but the prawns aren't bad with a little tartar sauce." Still holding my gaze, he guides my hand behind the shielding newspaper to rest against the crotch of his shorts, dragging my fingers along the very substantial geography of the cock beneath. As I gasp my admiration, he offers a knowing smile. "Thought you might like to know."

I give him a little squeeze. "I appreciate the tip," I say. "I'll keep that in mind."

He thanks the waitress, offers me a slight nod, then turns and walks out into the steamy night.

PLEASURE'S APPRENTICE

Remittance Girl

Above the venerable silver shop in the Burlington Arcade, he taught her the uses of pleasure; not the nervous-handed, spring-loaded fumbling of teenage lust, or the ego-abraded outcomes of young love.

Mr. Pierce offered Rebecca schooling in something quite different.

After quitting an English degree halfway through the first term, alienated by the prospect of having to read and deconstruct *Waiting for Godot* in French for the sake of authenticity, Rebecca Holloway found herself, both directionally and financially, at a loss.

Near Earl's Court, she rented a drab bedsit with diurnally cyclical smells. In the morning it inevitably stank of burnt toast. At midday it was redolent with the smell of bleach. And, by nightfall, every rental room in the house was infused with the ghost of overboiled cabbage.

Having only ever had a Saturday job selling trendy clothes

for pocket money, the possibility of full and gainful employment was daunting for Rebecca, but a lowering of expectations and a careful scanning of the ads in the evening newspaper paid off. Within a week, she found a position as silver-polisher and part-time shop assistant at Holmes & Sons Silversmiths in an arcade just off Bond Street. It was neither her previous work experience nor her successfully completed A-levels that got her the job. It was the fact that her antiquarian father had taught her how to decipher hallmarks and how to tell solid from plate—a skill she hadn't dreamed would ever come in handy.

There was, of course, no Mr. Holmes or Mr. Holmes junior. The business's name and stock had been sold on long ago to another proprietor with a less auspicious surname. The Ms. Patel who interviewed her made it clear that Rebecca's chief job was to assist Mr. Pierce in polishing the silver as it tarnished, make minor repairs and otherwise remain scarce. She was only to be seen on the shop floor at the morning and afternoon delivery of tea to the salespersons, and during the lunchtime lull when the sales assistants took their lunch. Otherwise, she should remain invisible on account of her dyed-purple hair and the ring in her nose, which didn't bring the right "tone" to the establishment.

The low-ceilinged room above the shop was dark. Light crept in from two small windows that let out onto the upper levels of an arcade that was almost Tudor in age. Night and day, summer and winter, the workspace was lit by a string of bare bulbs that ran down the ceiling of the tunnel-like room. The walls were unevenly plastered in that way you only see in black-and-white movies, and down one of the long walls stood a massive set of shelves groaning under the weight of row upon row of old silver: Georgian, Victorian, Edwardian, Art Nouveau and Deco. There was no new silver. Holmes & Sons had ceased to be silversmiths long ago. Now they were the Aladdin's cave of everything your mother didn't want to have to polish. Roughly in the center of the room was a long, wide wooden worktable, half covered in newspaper and laden with all manner of silver objects in need of attention. There were two chairs, opposite each other at the table, reminding Rebecca of the sort you saw in paintings of old schoolhouses—wooden, upright and mean.

In this domain—Mr. Pierce's preserve—he showed her how to set out the silver tea service and place the spoons onto the china cups and saucers in rigid gridlike order. On first meeting him, Rebecca thought he would have made the perfect butler in a murder mystery; he was a tallish, thickset man of about fifty, with a pale complexion and graying hair cropped close to his skull. His eyes were grayish blue and held a look of perpetual disinterest. He seldom spoke in sentences, and preferred to pass on his knowledge by showing rather than explaining. It was an approach he took to everything, Rebecca was later to learn.

The first day on the job, he sat at the large wooden work-table across from her and watched in solemn taciturnity as she polished teapots, salvers, trays and flatware. Then, he repolished every item. At ten thirty sharp he prepared the tea and gave her the huge, rattling tray to take down the narrow stairs, carpeted and threadbare, that lead to the shop floor. "They'll have finished," he muttered, at eleven, and sent her back down to retrieve the tea tray.

In turn, Rebecca sat and watched him as he tied an unnecessary apron around his waist and carefully washed the tea things at an ancient stone sink in the corner of the room.

She had never met a man like Mr. Pierce. His existential economy of words, of movement, of expression fascinated her. Her father had been a nervous and excitable man with a penchant for overdramatizing the banal. Her boyfriend in secondary school had been loud, sporty and prone to fits of temper. The lover she'd taken at university—a fellow student—had been melancholy and furtive, one moment bemoaning the injustice of the legal system and the next demanding proclamations of undying love. Mr. Pierce was a very different sort of man.

At first his silence intimidated her. He never told her she was polishing silver the wrong way. He simply polished it again. After a week of this redundancy of labor, Rebecca gathered up the courage to express her frustration.

"Mr. Pierce, if I'm not doing it right, tell me how you'd like it done."

This elicited a single word. He reached over the table, took the Victorian sterling milk jug from her hands and said: "Watch."

In the afternoons, Mr. Pierce would do repairs at the other end of the worktable. With torch, goggles and gloves, he would solder handles, spouts and knops back into their places. He would reset hinges and unbend ornamentation. After hours of sitting and watching, Rebecca asked if there was anything she could do, and was told she could read him the newspaper while he worked. On Thursdays, they sat together in silence and listened to the horse race reportages on an old brown melamine radio, used solely for that purpose, it seemed. Other times, it glowered silently at her from its spot on the shelf between the racks of flatware and the decorative picture frames.

Only after three weeks did Mr. Pierce allow her to make the tea. He supervised her in silence as always and, once she'd settled the teapot onto the tray, he nodded his approval.

"You'll put me out of a job, lass," he said, and indicated with a nod of his head that she could take it down to the shop.

Rebecca very much doubted there was anyone with the balls to consider firing Mr. Pierce. And it was with an inexplicable glow of pride that she carried the tea tray down to the sales staff.

In retrospect, Rebecca attempted but failed to comprehend

how, as time went by, her world contracted by inches, until the pattern of it was broken only by weekend visits with old school friends and the occasional trip to the cinema. Her life became a badly lit cycle of evenings spent reading in her bedsit, days in the workshop and the commute between the two. And equally incomprehensible was why it didn't bother her. Even as she watched it happen, knowing it was happening, there didn't seem anything unnatural in it. What mattered was that the tea was made correctly, the silver was polished properly and the public library was still open by the time she got off the bus after work. Her phone never rang, and the small portable television that came with the room offered her nothing that engaged her attention.

Then, one day, almost three months after her arrival at Holmes & Sons, something happened. Having retrieved the tray at 3:30 p.m. on a chilly November afternoon, Rebecca went to the stone sink and began to wash up. She stood at the sink, washing out a cup when she heard—or rather felt—Mr. Pierce step behind her.

"Aren't you forgetting something, lass?"

She glanced down to watch his arms reach around her waist. He placed one hand on her lower stomach and moved her back from the sink and against his big body. With the other, he draped the drab green apron around her and, smoothing it flat, he stepped away and tied its strings tight about her waist, leaving behind the mixed scent of lead solder, silver polish and masculinity.

The moment was electric. Her hand holding the china cup shook. Blood rushed up her chest and climbed the sides of her neck, making her skin burn. Her nipples stiffened into a sudden, awful ache. At her cunt, she felt a blossom of heat and then the creeping wetness seep into the crotch of her panties.

And that evening, having reached her cramped, shabby bedsit, she pulled off the still-damp panties, flung herself onto her single bed and masturbated her way to a panting, sobbing orgasm. She came with an intensity she had never experienced before. Not that she'd ever come with anyone else; neither of her lovers had had the skill or the inclination to uncover the mysteries of a body she hardly understood herself.

Why Mr. Pierce had elicited this extreme reaction was unfathomable. Rebecca only knew that he had. And so, at eleven the following morning, once she had brought up the tray and prepared to do the washing up, she knowingly and deliberately did not put on the apron. Sponge in one hand, dirty cup in the other, she stood at the sink apronless and waited.

The water from the faucet was icy. Her fingers numbed. But, after what seemed to Rebecca like an inordinately long pause, she felt him come up behind her, and do exactly what he'd done the day before.

"Forgetful, are we?"

"Yes. Sorry."

But she wasn't sorry in the least. All she could feel was his massive hand moving her into his meaty warmth and the efficient tug of the apron strings as he crossed them around her waist and tied them at her back.

Did that hand linger just a little longer over her belly? Did he take just a little more time in smoothing the apron in place? Did he tug the strings a little more snugly than he had the previous afternoon? The intensity of her arousal and the fog in her head made it impossible to know for sure.

It was Thursday, race day. The radio's nasal drone gave out the progress of the horses as they sped around the track at Kempton, as Rebecca came upstairs with the tray and set it by the sink. At first, she thought that Mr. Pierce was so engrossed in the narrative, he probably wouldn't notice as she washed the cups. But, having left off the apron, she set about her task. As she began to soap the second cup, she felt him behind her again.

This time he said nothing. All she heard was a slow, long exhalation. The hand again, encircled her waist, settled itself just below her navel and eased her back from the sink, against his body. But instead of moving to wrap the apron around her, he left it there. His heat seeped through her blouse, her skirt. And her body, realizing this was a breaking of the pattern, set her heart thundering in her chest. He pressed harder and she heard him inhale. The breath was uneven and stuttered as he drew it.

It seemed to Rebecca that he held her like that for an eternity, but it couldn't have been more than a few seconds. She had the sensation that somehow, she'd just stepped off a ledge and into thin air. It lingered until, with her ass pressed tight against his hips, she felt the slow and strangely frightening press of his cock as it came alive. With his free hand, he covered her breast easily. At first the pressure was warm, gentle, but it grew into something demanding and raw. He squeezed until she squirmed, and, when she did, his other hand pushed down the front of her skirt, massive fingers wedging into the space between her legs and cupping her roughly.

Rebecca had been so worked up even before Mr. Pierce had touched her that she almost came apart in his hands.

"Put down the cup, lass. Turn off the water." His voice was soft, almost inaudible above the radio's drone. Unsteadily, she lowered the cup into the sink and shut off the ancient faucet with a shaking hand. He held her there, letting her feel his erection throb against the clothed cleft of her ass. The hard metal of his belt dug into her backbone as she did what she was told. Then, without any warning, the grip on her breast eased and the hand at her groin disappeared. He took her shoulders, moving her away from the sink.

"I'll wash up today," he said and, without glancing at her, stepped up to the sink and began to soap the cups and saucers. For a moment, Rebecca stood in stunned silence, searching his impassive profile, glancing down at the dishes and then back up at Mr. Pierce.

"Go on then, there's all that Georgian flatware to be seen to. Don't stand about."

It was the most he'd ever said to her. With her heart still racing, and her body still wanting, and the echo of his fierce hands on her flesh, she returned to the table, sat down and finished her work.

Once the race commentary was over, Mr. Pierce switched off the radio, and they worked in silence until five-thirty. As her body cooled down and the hush stretched out, a sense of shame replaced the arousal.

Only when he followed her through the darkened interior of the closed shop and let her out the door, locking it behind them, did he speak.

"It's not a game," he said, his stern, gray eyes meeting hers as he pocketed the keys and pulled on a pair of gloves.

"No," she replied, unable to move in the pin of his gaze.

His face softened and he reached up, swiping the side of her cheek with a gloved finger. "You're awfully young, lass. Find yourself a nice young man."

There was no way to say what she wanted. She only knew that she did want, and with a terrible ferocity. Rebecca turned and fled down the arcade as if her body would burst apart into a thousand pieces if she didn't use it to run.

Friday morning found Rebecca in an only slightly calmer state. She had hardly slept the night before. All she could see when she closed her eyes was the old stone sink, the running faucet and the cup shaking in her hand. All she could feel was the overwhelming need Mr. Pierce engendered in her. All she could remember was the brief enormity of his touch. No one had ever held her with such purpose. For those fleeting minutes, when her body had quivered like liquid, she had never felt such a sense of being possessed in her life.

Throughout their morning work, she felt Mr. Pierce's stare. He watched everything she did. And under that unrelenting gaze, she dropped salvers and spilt polish and fumbled the simplest tasks.

"Take it down," he said, when the morning tea was ready.

She was sure she'd drop the tray as she brought it into the shop. And as the minutes ticked by, from ten thirty until eleven, a great battle raged in her mind. But when she walked back up the stairs with the empty cups, she had decided. Very deliberately, she put the tray beside the sink. And very deliberately she turned on the water and squeezed a generous amount of washing up liquid onto the scrubber. And very deliberately, she began to wash the dishes without the wearing the apron.

Mr. Pierce had watched her the entire time, from his seat at the worktable. He didn't move. "Lass, put the apron on," he said softly. Rebecca didn't glance at him. She stared down at the saucer in her hand and washed it with a furious purpose.

"Put it on."

His voice was close, but she didn't look up. Her blood was singing with an eerie defiance. Her flesh was on fire. Inside, muscles fluttered wildly, and the crotch of her panties was sodden with need. Hardly touching, Mr. Pierce reached around her and turned off the tap. He covered her hands with his and guided them down to the bottom of the sink. She let the plate clatter to the stone and dropped the sponge.

"Good lass." It was a soft, whisper close to her ear. Without releasing them, he guided both her hands to the thick, rough lip of the sink and forced her fingers to grip it. Then he let them go.

"Don't move. Not a word. Not a sound," he growled. The hands settled on her waist and then moved upward, big and sure. They took her like territory. As they covered her breasts, she flinched and heard his breath hitch. He was behind her, breathing hard, one hand groping her right breast while the other unbuttoned her blouse and pulled it open. He didn't bother to fight with her bra, simply tugged the cups down and the straps dug and burned at her shoulders as he took a breast in each hand and squeezed them. His big, rough fingers burrowed into her skin. At her back, she could feel the want bleed from his body. His hard-on pushed into the roundness of her ass, ground against her and unsteadied her, and he growled again.

"Not an inch. I told you."

Rebecca gripped the sink, steadied her body and closed her eyes. She clamped her mouth shut to stifle the moan that she was sure would emerge unbidden, but it was like trying to stop boiling water from bubbling. His hands moved down, leaving her nipples throbbing. They paused to grip her hips and hold her steady as he rubbed against her, before one snatched at her skirt and pulled it up. Fingers raked up the nylon of her stockings and past them, over bare thigh, and covered her sodden mound.

He made a noise, soft and low in his throat. "Is this for me, lass?"

The contact made it impossible to be still. Rebecca rocked her hips, drove herself against the hand at her crotch. "You know it is." It came out like slurry. Was it for him? For him specifically? For a man more than twice her age who never flirted, never wooed her, hardly spoke? And did any of that matter once she felt him tug her knickers down her thighs, once she heard him unbuckling his belt, unzipping himself? She listened to his trousers, keys in the pocket, slither and drop to the floor. The way he moved her to his liking, the delicious heat of him when he pushed his cock between her thighs and angled himself so expertly for the first, deep thrust. The way he bent over, bending her too, and braced himself against the same cold stone sink with one hand, the other clamped over her mound.

She had been so ready for him, for what seemed like so many days. When he finally took what she was offering, it only took half a dozen thrusts to detonate the bomb inside her. As if he'd done this many times before, he knew, and shushed her as she came on his cock. And so what should have been a cacophony of pleasure came out as a stream of choked off whimpers.

"Good lass," he panted. "Give me another." The hand that had steadied her pubic bone moved, fingers searched out and found her swollen clit. He coaxed it with each inward thrust, so that each felt like a stubborn door being battered open. And it was impossible to refuse him what he asked for. He fucked her methodically, meticulously. Rebecca could feel the ridge of his cock head as he withdrew almost completely before plunging home again. If he was worried about being caught fucking his assistant, he didn't fuck like he gave a damn. He fucked like he did everything else: quietly, carefully, thoroughly, until she broke again in shudders and sobs locked up in her chest. Only then did he come, as if he'd been waiting to see that she'd done the job properly before moving on to the next step. It wasn't quick or furtive. He just stopped thrusting and erupted into her cunt, letting her feel each hot spurt flood her passage. Then he withdrew, pulled her panties up roughly and put his trousers back on.

"Stand up, turn around." With the lassitude that comes from orgasm, Rebecca straightened herself and watched, mutely, while he repositioned her bra, and buttoned up her blouse. "Lots of work waiting. Better get to it, now."

In the days that followed, Rebecca learned a lot. Mr. Pierce taught her how to clean off broken pieces of silver, coat the sheared edges in flux and solder them back into place.

He also taught her how to please him. His huge hand wrapped around hers as she stroked his cock, using her saliva and his precome to make it slick. He showed her when he was ready for her, on her knees, looking up at him, to cover the head with her mouth and staunch the flood that resulted.

"Don't make a mess, lass," he said. He showed her how to ride him as he sat on one of the two schoolroom chairs. How to let him use her body the way he wanted, to relax as he guided her hips up and down. How to stifle her cries against the side of his neck when she came so hard from his use. Bent over the work-table, she was taught to lie still and silent and let him plunder her cunt and her ass with his fingers, his cock and his mouth. He never kissed her. Never said words of love to her. Never asked her out or did any of the things that lovers do. All he ever offered her was the pleasure of being possessed by him in that drab room above the shop. She never learned his first name.

When she left, a year later, to have another go at a university degree, she left knowing exactly what her body could do and with an unnatural reaction to the scent of silver polish.

THE NYLON CURTAIN

Elizabeth Coldwell

All he wanted was for me to wear stockings. When you consider all the proposals he could have made, this seemed mild. Innocent, even.

I'd answered his advert because it seemed so much less blatant than most of the others on the website. I wasn't looking for—or offering—no-strings sex. I wanted something quirky, something memorable; the ideal basis for a chapter or two in the book I planned to write. That's how you make your name these days: you spend a year dating only men you meet online or working as a high-class escort, rush out a book of your experiences and the next thing you know, you have a late-night TV documentary series. I was ambitious enough to see that as a path worth taking, but I needed the right angle.

The advert had requested a woman with "perfect pins." I wasn't sure I'd class my legs as perfect, but they were certainly good. I received enough admiring glances whenever I wore a short skirt to make that obvious. My figure wasn't bad, either. I sent the advertiser a photo of myself in a bikini on the beach at Brighton to prove it. No money would change hands, so neither of us was being exploited—unless getting someone to share all the intimate details of his special peccadillo with you, then writing about it for your own benefit was exploitation. I tried not to think of that as I squeezed myself onto a Northern Line train in the early evening rush hour, gussied up like a respectable Forties-era housewife, on my way to meet a man with an overwhelming appreciation for fully fashioned stockings.

Mr. Torrance, as I knew him, had been very insistent on the way I was to dress. I found a suitable jacket and skirt in a local charity shop, teaming it with a short-sleeved white blouse. Underneath that, he requested plain, functional white knickers, a suspender belt and stockings. Not owning a suspender belt, preferring instead the ease of slipping into tights, I borrowed one from my flatmate's underwear drawer. There were so many frilly, frothy pieces of nothing crammed in there I reckoned she wouldn't even notice it had gone. I felt rather self-conscious as I trotted down to the station on my highest heels, but this was London, after all, where it can be so much harder than you would think to draw attention to yourself.

The address I'd been given was on a quiet Islington street, not far from the Regent's Canal. Though the house was modest in size, tucked in the middle of a Georgian terrace, I suspected it was worth an eye-watering amount of money. I knew very little about Mr. Torrance, and how he was able to afford such a desirable home; we hadn't disclosed much in the way of personal information in the correspondence we'd shared up to this point. Nothing he'd told me, however, had given the impression he was in any way odd or dangerous: naturally, he was a little obsessive when it came to the subject of stockings, but men could be exactly the same about their football team or their favorite rock band. It didn't necessarily make them individuals to be avoided.

I patted my hair, which I'd pinned up in what I hoped was a suitably authentic style, and hesitated with my finger on his doorbell. I still had the option of turning and leaving, but I'd put too much effort into my preparation not to at least see the effect it had on my online admirer.

I rang the bell and waited. Eventually, the door swung open. "Charlotte? I'm glad to see you're punctual. Do come in."

I stepped into the hall and took my first real look at Mr. Torrance. He must have been around fifty, twice my age, with closely cropped gray hair and striking, ice-blue eyes behind wire-rimmed glasses. He wore a dark, well-cut suit: if I thought it was a little strange that he hadn't even removed his jacket in his own house, I didn't say anything.

At his instruction, I followed him into the lounge. He told me to make myself comfortable while he fixed me a drink. "How would a gin sling suit you?"

"That sounds fine," I said, not wanting to admit I didn't know what a gin sling was, but suspecting it had been fashionable in the period around which Mr. Torrance's fantasies clearly revolved.

While he busied himself with the contents of his drinks cabinet, I looked round the room, trying to imprint as many details as I could on my memory. It wasn't a particularly memorable room, but its very ordinariness would provide the perfect contrast to the events I was intending to write about once I got home.

Mr. Torrance handed me a frosted martini glass and I took a sip of my drink: gin, mixed with sugar, soda water and a twist of lemon, as far as I could tell. Quite pleasant. A couple of these could lead a girl to all manner of indiscretions.

"Now, Charlotte, I'm sure you know why I asked you here, and I'm so pleased to see you dressed as I requested."

Mr. Torrance settled himself in an armchair opposite me. He had a glass of what looked like scotch on the rocks, and he took a drink before continuing. Despite his self-assured exterior, it almost seemed he was steadying his nerves. "Before we go any further, I'd like you to take off the stockings you're wearing now and put these on."

He handed me a slender packet. The old-fashioned typeface and cellophane that crackled at my touch told me this was the genuine article. Wolsey Skin-Tone Nylons in a shade described as Ranch Mink. Unworn stockings from sixty years ago, in their original packaging. I was almost afraid to unwrap them.

"Should I go into the bathroom and change, or—?"

"No, I'd like you to do it here. I want to watch you." So that was his thing. He was a voyeur. In that case, I would give him a show, despite the embarrassment I felt at hiking up my skirt in front of a virtual stranger till my stocking tops were on view.

He was shaking his head, and I wondered what I'd done wrong. "No, no, no," he sighed. "That suspender belt really isn't the thing at all. It needs to have proper metal clips, not those flimsy plastic things. But I suppose it will have to do for now."

He didn't say another word as I unclipped the ten-denier Lycra stockings I'd been wearing, rolled them down and off and carefully extracted the Wolseys from their packaging. Before I could go any further, he asked, "You did bring gloves like I asked you to?"

He'd been very firm on that point: I was to fetch a pair of white cotton gloves with me. When I nodded, he said, "I'd like you to put them on now, please. I'd hate you to snag those beautiful things."

Putting on stockings while you're wearing gloves isn't the

easiest task in the world, but I managed it, doing my very best to ensure the seams at the back were straight and the fashioned heel hugged my foot correctly. The nylon felt cool against the smooth skin of my legs, and I noticed it didn't cling in the same way as its Lycra-rich modern counterpart as I pointed my toes, admiring the way the stockings looked.

"Very nice." Mr. Torrance's voice was noticeably strained. "Now I'd like you to slip your shoes back on and walk up and down for me."

Taking another fortifying mouthful of my gin sling, I did as he asked. It was the strangest sexual experience I'd ever had—and it was sexual; the constant pulsing in my pussy and the way my sensible knickers were clinging wetly to my lips proved that, as did the bulge in Mr. Torrance's suit trousers. But not a word was said as I slowly paraded back and forth in front of him, elegant as any catwalk model. Whatever was happening in his imagination, he wasn't sharing it with me.

He didn't even ask me for another glimpse of my stocking tops; not on that occasion, anyway. Perhaps he really did find my suspender straps too offensive. I remedied that before my next visit, finding a shop in Soho that sold vintage-style lingerie. I left having purchased an appropriate suspender belt—white, to match my sensible knickers. It was three times as wide as the flimsy thing I'd borrowed from my flatmate, with six thick straps and all with the requisite metal fastenings.

The belt did the trick. This time, I was required to lie back on the sofa and raise my legs in the air, one straight, one bent at the knee. In that pose, Mr. Torrance couldn't fail to get a good look at what was beneath my skirt. I assumed he liked what he saw, because he began to talk.

Gradually, he filled me in on the little details of his fetish. Only the genuine article turned him on. Although any number of shops, like the one I'd visited, stocked fully-fashioned nylons, they were reproductions. Some of them were almost as good as the real thing, produced on machines from the Forties and Fifties to the exact specifications of those I wore, but they just weren't the same. There were many men, he told me, whose craving for stockings would stop being satisfied for good the day the last original pair was laddered to the point where it was no longer wearable.

He spent much of his free time searching for stockings, trawling Internet auction sites and vintage clothing shops and snapping up as many pairs as he could. As he talked, I learned about the great fetish models of the past, like Bettie Page, who according to Mr. Torrance had no equal, and the photographers who'd captured glorious leg shots with obsessive detail—Elmer Batters, Irving Klaw and the rest. All of it was valuable material for the pages of text building up on my netbook, describing my visits to the house in Islington.

A couple of times as he talked he stroked my stocking-clad legs, as though to emphasize a point, but that was all the contact we had. Despite that, the sexual tension in the room was almost stifling. I wondered whether Mr. Torrance masturbated once I left after one of these sessions. I certainly did. Once I was back home, I'd rush to my room, lock the door and undress till I was wearing nothing but the vintage suspender belt and my cheap supermarket stockings. Then I would stand in front of the mirrored wardrobe door, slip a finger between my legs and rub my clit till I came, knees buckling, body wracked with sobs.

I'd never had orgasms as intense as the ones I experienced after a visit to Mr. Torrance. As I caressed myself, I pictured him stripped of the sober suit I'd never actually seen him remove, gripping his hard cock in his hand and wanking himself with short, frantic movements of his fist, till come sprayed out over his fingers.

Gradually, I began to make little breakthroughs in my relationship with him. The first came when he asked me to remove my skirt at the start of one of our sessions. From the waist up, I was still utterly respectable, but now I sat in my stockings and underwear, pretending not to be aware of the way his eyes burned into the pale band of flesh above the thick welts of the latest pair of stockings he'd acquired for me to wear.

From him, I learned more than I'd ever known—or thought I'd want to know—about the art of manufacturing stockings. The seam was an integral part of the fully fashioned nylon, designed to hold the stocking together. Only over time had it acquired the unutterably sensual connotations so many men saw in that line running straight and true up the back of a woman's leg.

He began to talk in ever more personal terms, too. He revealed that he'd never been married, though he'd had any number of girlfriends over the years. Most of them, however, had been unable to comprehend his fascination for stockings, or his insistence that they wear them in and out of the bedroom. Only one woman had seemed able to cope with his fetish, seeming not to mind that sex would never be truly satisfying for him unless nylons were involved. He would have married her, but for one thing—she had what he described as stumpy legs and thick ankles. "Call me shallow," he said, "but I really wouldn't have minded if she had an ugly face. I could have lived with that. In the end, it all came down to the fact I just couldn't stand her ugly legs."

Finally, he'd decided the only way to satisfy his craving was to use escorts. Whenever he managed to acquire a pair of genuine vintage nylons, he called a certain agency and booked a girl for the evening—specifying, naturally, that she must have perfect legs. For the last couple of years he'd seen the same woman every time, a Russian named Natalia, who'd trained with the Bolshoi ballet but failed to make it as a dancer. "Her legs," he sighed. "So supple, so slender, so exquisite." Unfortunately, she tired of the escort business, having earned enough money to go back to Moscow and live in comfort. Since then, there had been no one—until me.

I wanted to ask why he'd placed the advert; if he'd been happy to reduce his sex life to a series of commercial transactions, why this new arrangement? No cash changing hands, but no sex, either. I sensed there might be more he wanted to tell me, but I knew I'd have to wait until he felt comfortable.

Then came the night when I was lying on his cream leather sofa, carelessly trailing a finger toward my stocking top and I glanced over to see that Mr. Torrance—or Jonathan, as he'd recently started allowing me to call him—had unzipped his fly and extracted his cock.

I was wearing a new combination of lingerie for the first time, one to which he'd treated me.

He'd given a gift-wrapped package to me the last time I visited him, pressing it into my hands as I stood on the doorstep saying my good-byes and telling me not to open it till I got home. When I did, I discovered it contained a suspender belt almost identical to the one I usually wore, only in black, and a pair of black knickers with sheer organza panels front and back. When I tried them on, I discovered these panels gave saucy glimpses of the cleft between my bumcheeks and my thick pubic bush. As Jonathan had impressed on me that the stockings came from a time before the salon wax and the battery-powered epilator, I'd been cultivating a more natural look. I even treated my newly luxuriant muff to the odd squirt of conditioner in the bath.

By this time, I suspected I was developing my own little obsession for nylons. Nothing on the scale of Jonathan's, naturally, but when the autumn fashions started appearing in the shops and the pencil skirt came back in vogue, I relished the opportunity it gave me to dress in stockings and heels on a regular basis. I was changing, I knew that. I no longer worried that when I walked down the street in my Forties regalia I would be mocked as the missing member of the Andrews Sisters. It didn't matter what anyone else thought: I felt confident, sexy, in control.

So it came as no surprise to see my latest display had caused Jonathan to finally give up some of his own rigid self-control and start playing with himself. I pretended not to have noticed, though, as his hand continued to stroke the length of his erection. He had a nice-looking cock, from the glimpse I'd had, and I wished it was my hand straining to meet around its thickness. Instead, I let my fingers stray carelessly over the crotch of my knickers, wanting to touch myself but needing a direct instruction from the man who watched me so intently before I felt sure I could proceed. I kept thinking of one of his earliest emails to me: "All I want you to do is wear stockings." As far as I knew, that was still all he wanted me to do. So I continued to tease him—and myself—as his breathing became harsher, more audible, and the room resounded to the soft slapping noises of his hand on his cock. I didn't even look around when he groaned out loud and came. By the time I finally pulled myself back into a sitting position, he was zipped up and respectable once more, the crumpled tissue on the table beside him the only indication of what had just happened.

When I got home that night, there was no pretense, no teasing. I was desperate to come, turned on beyond belief by my meeting with Jonathan. I kept a couple of vibrators in my bedside drawer. One was a discreet little thing that looked more like a computer mouse than a sex toy; designed to apply gentle but insistent stimulation to the clitoris, it never let me down. The other was a beast of a vibrator, longer and thicker than any cock I'd encountered in reality. I'd bought it back in my student days when a friend and I had paid a giggly, "aren't we daring?" visit to a sex shop, and I had to be really, really aroused to take it without discomfort. Tonight I was ready for it. I reached for the beast and a bottle of lube, getting the thing slippery wet. Gently but firmly, I eased it up inside me, feeling it stretch me to a point that was bordering on painful, but not caring. I needed to be filled. As I got more used to the feel of it, I relaxed, slowly working the dildo in and out while I pictured Jonathan Torrance fucking me, his big body on top of mine and my stocking-clad legs wrapped round his back so he could stroke them. The image was so vivid it was only moments before I was coming, one finger on my clit and the obscenely fat sex toy pushed in me as far as it would go.

As I lay panting, shattered by the strength of my climax, I knew I had to find out whether sex with Jonathan would be as good as I imagined it. Everything was moving to the point where our relationship would become more than one revolving around talk and tease, I was sure, and I was determined to make it happen sooner rather than later.

The following Friday, I received an email from Jonathan. "I have something very special for you," it said, "and I need to see you as soon as possible." I'd made plans to go out with a couple of girlfriends that night, but nothing that couldn't easily be put off till another time. I was dying to know what Jonathan's "something special" was, but I also knew that compared to a night of modeling stockings for him, clubbing with the girls held no appeal.

I sensed the mood was different the moment I stepped into

Jonathan's hallway. He seemed as excited as a small boy on Christmas morning, and I quickly learned why. He mixed me a sidecar as part of his ongoing quest to educate me about classic cocktails, then reached for a packet that lay on the coffee table.

"Aristoc Harmony Point." His tone was hushed, reverent. "These are the Holy Grail of stockings. I've been waiting so long to find a pair in your size. You wouldn't believe how many so-called burlesque dancers I had to outbid to own these."

I was reaching for my gloves before he'd even handed the stockings over, not needing to be told to treat these stockings with the respect Jonathan clearly believed they deserved. Having gone through the ritual of removing my everyday stockings, I gently eased the vintage beauties out of their packaging. Aware of Jonathan greedily watching my every move, I slowly rolled them up my legs and clipped them into place. The sheer, silky material, in a shade of gray the packaging described as Gentle Smoke, hugged the contours of my legs beautifully. I didn't even have to glance up to know Jonathan approved of the sight.

Down came my skirt, to give Jonathan an uninterrupted view of my stocking tops. He sighed. "Oh, yes. Pose for me, Charlotte. Show those wonderful stockings off."

I did as he asked, twisting on his sofa to display the hosiery to best effect. I was sure I wasn't as poised or as supple as Natalia, the former ballerina, had been when she'd modeled for Jonathan, but I hoped he was enjoying my efforts.

"I want you to do something for me," Jonathan said. "I want you to take your knickers off."

I hurried to obey, wondering if he'd been saving this request until he was in possession of a pair of Harmony Point stockings. Letting my knickers drop to the floor, I went to stand close to him, so he could get a good look at my bushy pussy, framed by the thick suspender straps.

As I'd expected, he'd opened his fly and freed his cock. Gazing at his mouthwatering erection, I couldn't hold back any longer. We'd been playing this game for months now, and I was more than ready to take it to the next level.

Straddling Jonathan's lap, I caught hold of his hand, keeping his cock nice and steady so I could sink down on to it. "Charlotte, please," he murmured. I put my finger to his lips, wriggling till he was lodged snugly inside me. He felt as though he belonged there, and I began to fuck him, shifting up and down slowly.

"Touch my beautiful stockings," I urged him, placing his hands on my thighs so he could do just that. He seemed a little reluctant at first, but as I rocked faster he started to move with me. His hands moved from my legs to my bumcheeks, pulling me down harder on to his cock. Occasionally, I felt the cold teeth of his zip against my tender flesh, but it just added to the thrill. There was something deliciously decadent about fucking a man who hadn't even undressed, who just had his cock poking out of his trousers, and I was relishing it. The stockings were making sensual slithery noises as they rubbed against his legs, and I pressed my mouth to his in a hard, probing kiss. I was in charge here, Jonathan following my lead as we both moved to orgasm. I dropped a hand between my legs so I could stroke my clit. Fiery sparks shot through me, and I closed my eyes and surrendered to my climax. If I'd had the strength, I would have climbed off Jonathan so that when he came, I could direct his spunk over my stockings, but all I could do was cling to him as he bucked and groaned, ejaculating up into me.

When I finally let his cock slip out of me, I made to kiss him again, but he pushed me away.

"How could you?" he asked. "I never asked you to fuck me."

"But you didn't exactly say no," I replied. "You can't tell me you didn't enjoy that. I mean, didn't you fuck Natalia, and the other girls you paid to wear stockings for you?"

To my surprise, he shook his head. "Never. That was the arrangement we had. It was never about sex, Charlotte. It was about the stockings. They understood that. I thought you did, too."

So this is it, I thought, as I got dressed. *This is where it ends.* Confused as I was by what had just happened, I still made sure to fold his precious stockings neatly, fearful of laddering them. How ironic that when this all started, I'd never intended to have sex with him. I'd never intended to develop any kind of attachment to him; I was simply going to get the material I needed for my book, then walk away. Instead, I'd got hooked. Hooked on the game. More importantly, hooked on him. I knew now why things had always moved at his pace; because I hadn't been the one in control, no matter what I thought. Jonathan had, and because that hadn't been enough for me, I'd crossed the line. We couldn't go back to the way things had been before, I was sure of that.

As I quietly closed the front door behind me, I realized I didn't even care about the wretched book. All I cared about was Jonathan, and now I'd lost him.

For weeks after that, I couldn't bear even to look at a pair of stockings. I pushed my Forties outfits and vintage underwear to the back of the wardrobe, and took to dressing in little strappy tops and jeans, the outfits I'd favored before I met Jonathan. I went on a couple of dates with one of my flatmate's friends, but my heart wasn't in it. I'd got off on the thrill of dressing for Jonathan, of posing for him, of being part of his all-consuming fetish, and now there was a big hole in my life I didn't see any other man ever filling.

Then I came home one evening to find a small, flat package in the post, addressed in handwriting I didn't recognize. I opened it to find a pair of Harmony Point stockings in my size. There was a note. "Charlotte, I've been foolish. I thought I only needed the stockings, but I realize now I need what we had—what we still could have. I'll understand if you send these back unworn, but I would very, very much prefer it if you walked through my door with them adorning your perfect pins. I'll be waiting. Jonathan."

I hugged the stockings to my chest. If I hurried, I could be to Jonathan's by eight. Thanking whichever deity decides that sometimes people deserve a second chance, I went to hunt for my suspender belt.

A BIG DECK

Rosalía Zizzo

"POKER NIGHT!" Angela hears male shouting, beer bottles clanging and chairs skidding across the floor as the usual crew settles in one Friday night for a routine game of cards. She passes through the foyer and into the dining area where everyone is preparing to get drunk, make some money and have a great time—very much like last week's affair. And the week before that. Inhaling deeply, Angela pulls a chair out and slides quietly into the seat, realizing she is the only female again amidst a horde of men who have been marinated in testosterone. *Get ready*, she thinks. *You've always fit in. Always. Even with Scott in the room.* Scott is really the reason she returns each week, with freshly shaven, moisturized legs and a churning stomach. He's the reason for dabbing on a wee bit of rose-colored lipstick and for wearing an informal floral skirt, flared around the thighs, to an event that calls for jeans. And he's the reason for that spritz of perfume as she's heading out the door.

Charlie sits in the dealer seat as always, Larry next to him, then silent Jackson, and then the man of her fantasies, Scott—the ringleader of Friday's three-ring circus—who sits smiling up at her, revealing clean, white teeth. She glances at those soft hands she imagines cupping her upturned face to lift her lips to his. She takes a deep breath and looks under her lashes at him, the hunky alpha male with green eyes and sandy-blond hair, and tries hard not to picture him without clothes.

"Hey, Mr. Modesty. How's the big deck?" Angela says and meets Scott's eyes, gazing directly into them with a closed-mouth smile. She's pointing out his unintended reference to his large stack of cards last week, and she chuckles quietly—ignoring her skipping heartbeat while slyly smirking at the intended pun and at Scott's shocked expression. His growing pink flush belies his traditionally cocky attitude she sees every Friday at poker night. In the past, just like today, she feels that twang zap her gut every time she looks in his direction and sees his strong jaw and smooth, rounded muscles. Charlie continues dealing over the snorts and snickers and arms reaching for handfuls of pretzels and chips. The guys appreciate that Angela behaves like one of them, and although she remains unaware of his interest, Scott enjoys the fact that Angela's long, dark hair and dark eyes, not to mention her smooth, tan legs, add an air of mystery to their otherwise masculine evening.

"Ohhh," the guys shout in unison. After fidgeting and attempting composure, Scott fans out his cards in front of his face like a shield. He doesn't normally let anything get to him, especially a woman, so he quickly puffs himself up with that illusory, macho strength by lifting his chin and squaring his shoulders. He takes a brusque swig of beer and lowers the bottle, pounding it onto the table. Angela is prepared to see him thump on his chest with his fists like an ape.

Uncrossing her legs and holding her beer bottle like a cock,

Angela swallows a gulp of her drink while lifting the cards Charlie has dealt her. Scanning each card as she puts it into her hand, she runs her tongue over the lips of a crooked smile, looking very much like an Italian painting. She exhales for a full three seconds before straightening her back and lifting her shoulders higher, which makes her feel stronger with each passing minute. Lifting her eyes over her cards, she then asks, "Have you played with your big deck lately?" The crowd pauses only briefly, then hoots again while considering its cards. Looking at Scott's surprised reaction to her newly found, audacious humor, she reaches across the table quickly to pet his hand that has loosened and threatens to drop the cards onto the smudged wood. If she felt bold enough, she'd even pull him to her mouth so she could taste the drink from his lips. *Oh, gawd.*

Crossing her legs again, she grabs a couple of pretzels and brings them to her grinning mouth, poking her tongue out to taste the salt crystals that cover every curlicue. She pops one in her mouth and crunches, still grinning like a cat. After nudging Scott's arm with her elbow, she tilts her head back and tosses her hair while sweeping a few tendrils away from her face.

"Well...uh..." Scott stammers.

"Are we playing with it tonight, Scotty?" shouts someone in a Scottish accent. Everybody laughs. It's the joke that keeps on giving, like the Energizer Bunny that keeps on clanging, even after a week has gone by. The guys slug each other in the shoulder and grab their own crotches, begging Scott to whip it out.

He mumbles something about Angela while glancing at her, confused. "What's gotten into you?" He sees her looking coyly at him from the corner of her eye, tucking her chin into her shoulder and hiding so that an explosive laugh doesn't escape her throat. Tiny beads of sweat appear at his temples. "Deck. I said, 'DECK' and I meant to say, 'deck.'" He can't keep the unusual whine out of his voice, which makes Charlie slam his beer down on the table before letting loose a loud guffaw that sends the rest of the gang into fits of laughter.

"So we're not playing with your big deck tonight?" Charlie glances above his own fanned cards, causing Angela to clap her hand over her mouth to prevent a burst of beer from spewing out.

"Aw, Scott. I'm sure you've got a handle on the situation, man. A FIRM grip." *More laughter.*

"Yeah. I know it must be HARD, but I think you have a HANDle on the situation."

"A FIRM hand."

"With a STROKE of luck, you could be an up and COMing senator," chimes in Larry.

"The tension is GROWING THICKer as we speak."

"You guys all have dirty minds."

Immediately, a male chimes in. "Of course we do, but I don't think you realized Angela had one, too." The more he fights it, the harder they rib him.

Watching such a gorgeous man squirm fills Angela with a deep sense of satisfaction. She feels the corners of her mouth turn upward as she swings her gaze in his direction. Maybe it is because he always looks so perfect, acts so superior and makes her feel so pitiful in his mighty presence whenever she is around him. Maybe the camaraderie of the group gives her the necessary strength. And maybe she just wants to see him prove to the crowd he has an item worthy of unquestionable praise.

Fantasies about feeling that velvety soft skin on her tongue swirl in her mind. She wants to lick the tip, tease the opening and taste the salt oozing from the hole. She even feels the heat rush through her stomach, move north to her cheeks and south to her pussy so that it opens and drips moisture into her panties.

She wiggles in her seat to stop the arousal, but it only increases her desire. She wants to hold the base of his cock and aim it toward her mouth so badly she feels butterflies gathering in her stomach as she swallows a mouthful of beer. *I want it now.*

"Okay. Okay. Let's get the game started. Let's play cards," she demands.

And then...he shakes his head and arms as if preparing for a wrestling match or a battle. Dropping his head right to his shoulder with a crack, then left, and popping his knuckles one by one, he manually shivers up his body. His eyes darken and his face converts back into the confident man they all know and Angela is used to. You can see the transformation take place like in a sci-fi movie when a beast converts back to its original human form...or the reverse.

"Let's play," he growls.

After an hour of turning over her meager fortune to the tribe of hooting cave dwellers, Angela throws in the towel, exhaling loudly.

"Looks like you lack the funds for witnessing my enormous manhood." He exaggerates a pout, giving her a look of superiority. "Too bad. So sad." Turning his laughing face to the ceiling, Scott tiptoes his fingers down Angela's forearm, grabs her hand and places it on his thigh, close to his rigid crotch.

"Oh, go fuck yourself," Angela says, as if offended, quickly yanking her hand away.

"I think I'd rather fuck YOU." He gives her a devilish look.

Oh no. He's doing it again. Her gut ties in knots. "I think I'm worthy of a little clemency," she states defiantly. "I'm the queen of this group, after all." *Her strength amazes her.*

"Yes, your hotness; I mean, highness." Scott displays his upturned palm and bows to a smirking Angela. "Shall I provide a throne?" He laughs. His upturned palm sweeps across the air. "It's in the bathroom."

Angela rolls her eyes.

"Show 'em," orders Charlie to a flurry of hands dropping their cards for all to see. "A pair of kings."

"Squat."

"Ace high."

"Three-of-a-kind."

"Uh, well, that's it for me," groans Angela. She flops her cards on the table. "I've got absolutely nothing. And I'm out of money. My wallet is a pocketful of lint. Anyone care to front me some cash?" She looks hopefully around the table, batting her lashes and pulling down a bit of shirt to expose her bare shoulder. Silence. Just as she sighs and gives up, reaching to the ground beside her chair to whisk her purse out the door, Scott catches her wrist.

"Is it time to make it more interesting?" He looks from man to man. "Angela's out of cash. Whatever shall we do?" He drips sarcasm from his mouth while clapping his palms on his cheeks, leaving a slapping noise and forming an O with his lips. All the men turn to him.

"Interesting how?" Charlie edges closer to Scott, elbows on the table. Scott displays a gleaming set of teeth that sparkle on a face that doesn't try to hide his mischief.

"Well..." He rubs his palms together. His eyes glimmer.

"Oh, never mind. I'm outta here." Angela turns to go, but Scott catches her arm again.

"Don't be scared. If we play an alternative to strip poker, you can make all your money back." He notices her shaking head. "No no no. Stop acting innocent already," he commands with a voice that could bring even the queen to her knees. "I know you're both a voyeur and an exhibitionist." Angela starts to deny it, but Scott cuts her off. "You've been looking at my crotch all evening, joking about it, and you relentlessly flirt and show your skin, so what'll it be?"

Sighing, Angela turns to him. "I'm listening."

"An article of clothing is cash. Just put it on the table like the money. You win? You keep it all, the money and clothing."

Looking at the men's attentive gaze awaiting her response, she groans in defeat. Deciding it sounds agreeable and better than being endlessly harassed, Angela nods. "All right. You're all drunk anyway so probably won't remember a thing tomorrow, and I wouldn't mind winning some cash back."

The guys all shout with joy: "Whoo hoo!" Excited, they scoot their chairs closer to the table while Charlie shuffles the cards.

"C'mon, darlin'. Ante up." Thinking she's figured out how to beat him at his own game, Angela stands and drops her panties to the floor. Everything else remains in place, so it doesn't look as if she has removed a stitch of clothing, and although her naked-ness is not visible, the guys become silent in their knowledge that a woman stands free and clear under her skirt in the dining room. She scoops up the slightly damp panties that smell of her arousal and tosses them smugly to the table. All faces turn to the undergarment, unceremoniously gawking, and her triumphant glow quickly fades when she sees all jaws go slack, and all eyes staring riveted to the pile of red silk crumpled on the table. They fix their gazes on the pile, spellbound.

"I guess she thought you said to PANTY up," mutters Charlie after a long pause. Everyone snickers weakly. Scott flashes a smile from the panties to Charlie to Angela without losing the authority to his face.

With a distracted group of males, Angela easily wins the first hand, and she shoots out of her seat, punching her fists into the air, jumping up and down, which bounces her breasts and wiggles her rear as part of her victory dance. Scott looks around the room and quickly dives between Angela's legs, flipping the ends of her skirt over the top of his head. His head buried under her skirt, he grips the globes of her ass and holds her body firmly to his face, which startles everyone, especially Angela.

"Whoa," Larry whispers.

Angela starts to protest and shove him away but stops and stares open-eyed when she feels him lick along the already open slit, making it impossible for him to resist diving into the open slash with his tongue, which slowly strokes each side of the clit, plunges into her cunt over the top of the clit and teases the base of the swelling gem, making it harden and throb. The pleasure keeps her anchored in place as she looks around the room. Sure, she's always been an exhibitionist, but gazing into multiple eyes, while someone's tongue finds her clit and his mouth sucks her labia, brings it to a whole new level. Her skirt lifts and drops like an umbrella opening and closing as he bobs his head up and down. She feels his hair on her crotch as he wiggles his head back and forth. Feeling his tongue swirl slow circles around her clit, she thrusts a bit toward Scott's face. She watches Larry and Jackson gape and start to unconsciously reach for their zippers in a daze. When Scott relaxes his tongue and slowly laps at her clit, Angela audibly releases a moan.

Every moment Angela remains spread to Scott's face makes him hungrier. He fucks her with his tongue, pushing it in and out so that it grazes each side, and from the noises escaping his throat, he savors this every bit as much as Angela does, increasing the tempo only when she hugs him to her and, whining, begs for more.

Aware that six eyes are on her, but drunk with desire, Angela places her palms on Scott's upper back that is covered by her skirt. She looks into all the glassy eyes as she feels Scott's tongue move in and out, rubbing both left and right along the inner walls of her cunt, slick with her juices and his saliva. She adjusts her feet so she feels stable, but she still rocks, weak-kneed. Each time Scott enters and exits with his tongue, he brushes against her clit, pushing the length of his tongue along the walls and pulling it out to the entrance. Angela clutches at her shirt, crinkling the ends upward so that her belly is exposed and then in desperation she frantically releases her shirt to squeeze her head between her hands. She thumps her forehead with the heel of her palm.

"Oh," she breathes. "Oh, oh, Scott."

As her orgasm starts its upward climb, she looks wildly about the room, searching for unspoken answers for her current predicament. She doesn't want Scott to stop but knows she should make him stop, and she cannot possibly make him finish until she finishes. She tenses her legs as he continues a steady pace toward her fulfillment. And then...he does stop, making Angela groan in dismay. *No.* Scott emerges from beneath Angela's skirt, his hair messy with moist ringlets and his face flushed and with a dewy glow. Juices glimmer at the corners of his mouth. Looking at him in amazement, Angela stares—breathless, startled and unsatisfied. He circles her waist with his fingers and lifts her to the table, twirling her lengthwise as the guys scramble out of their seats and clear the table of bottles and snacks. Scott forces her into a prone position and promptly begins where he left off by clamping his mouth around her mound and gorging on her clit. His warm lips surround her while his tongue moves deftly inside her. He sucks and licks her flesh in frantic need. When he adds a couple fingers to the mix, following his tongue with the digits' rapid pumping, she clutches her hair in tight fists.

Angela tenses her pussy, uncontrollably thrusting toward his face, and she envisions Scott's cock penetrating her again and again. She grasps fistfuls of hair and sucks her own tongue in desperation while she lifts her ass from the table repeatedly, silently pleading for more. And just when she thinks she can't take any more, she feels the weight drop before sailing upward through her pussy, her belly and her chest. She calls out his name as she erupts behind closed eyes, where white sparkles flash like fireworks in the sky. She releases the breath she hadn't realized she was holding until her lungs no longer feel painfully tight and her constricted chest slowly relaxes with a sigh. She feels Scott's tongue continue to lightly stroke her until she blows out a sigh in completion, and then she appears to drift to sleep.

Lips parted and clearly in shock, Charlie, Jackson and Larry all gaze at both of them, speechless. They all turn to one another, and the room stays silent for what seems an eternity as Scott raises his head.

Attempting to calm the sexual tension in the room and bring normalcy to the evening, Charlie breaks the silence by croaking, "So how's life at the office supply store, Angela?" He swipes his index finger across his upper lip and whispers, "Man I need a cold shower."

Angela blinks her eyes and stares at the chipped paint on the ceiling. It takes a while for her to think about Charlie's words and about work. As she sits up—disoriented, blinking, arranging her skirt and shirt, and raking her fingers through her hair—she breathes, "Um, okay, I guess." She moves her head vigorously from side to side and takes another deep breath while she feels her heartbeat wind down. "There's this computer lap dance that I've been eyeballing, and I like getting news of the most recent— what?" She notices lips twisted into grins around the table, but her mind is still too mixed up to put it all together. "Huh? How do you all get something out of a question like that?" The guys burst into laughter.

"I think I need to visit you at work," says Scott, who has risen to stand near her side and brushes an arm across his mouth.

Still in confusion she states, "I suppose you'll ask for a lap dance." Angela looks at him, awaiting his response.

"Sounds great, but don't you mean a lap DESK?" He grins, the sides of his mouth glistening with her juices.

"Oh." She looks around the room at all their upturned mouths. "Yeah."

BAD

Kay Jaybee

I'm a bad girl. That's what Con tells me when his belt hits my arse: when he's got me bending over the kitchen stool, my trousers around my ankles, my hands gripping its legs for all they're worth.

With each swipe of the leather strap he tells me I'm a whore, I'm naughty, I'm bad. And each time he strikes, each time the burn of the belt cuts through me I think, *YES! I am bad, I am a whore. I love it.*

I love that no one but him really knows me, that I'm just an ordinary middle-class thirtysomething woman in baggy jeans and a T-shirt, pushing her trolley around the supermarket like everyone else; sitting in her office typing up letters, cleaning the house, mowing the lawn—right up until I get a call telling me it's time to be bad.

I've got one of those posh phones that have a different ringtone depending on who calls or texts me. Whenever I hear the theme from *The Great Escape* I know it's him. My blood freezes, but at the same time, before the third note is even out, my heart rate has doubled and my hands chill while my body heats up.

I have a routine now. I don't look at the message instantly, and I give it at least four rings before I pick up, savoring the moment of contact itself, picturing Con on the other end of the call, anticipating my response. It is the only time I have the power to make him do the waiting.

Yesterday the call came when I was about to leave work. I'd already switched off my computer and was putting my coat on, contemplating whether I could be bothered to cook, or if I should grab a takeout on the way home. The second I felt the vibration of the phone in my pocket, accompanied by the familiar tune, my appetite disappeared—well, my appetite for food.

"Would you lick pussy for me?" The tone of his voice was normal, as if he was asking me if I'd like a cup of tea.

"Yes, of course; silly question." I was careful to keep my own voice light, very aware of my work colleagues still milling about the office. As I spoke, I could feel my pulse quicken, and my own voice was screaming at the back of my head: *Would you? Do you mean it?* I'd never done anything like that before, and even though I'd read a hundred girl-on-girl erotic stories, that didn't mean I'd ever seriously contemplated doing it for real.

That's how it is when he rings. He asks me to do something, and I say yes. It makes me feel good; powerful somehow, even though I'm unquestioningly a plaything to his sexual whims.

"I know a girl. Are you free this evening?" My palms felt sticky and my heart rate upped from a trot to a gallop.

I failed to keep the sudden fear that I was going to be replaced from my voice, "A girl?"

He laughed, "Don't panic! I don't mean a girl like you. No one is like you. No, this girl will teach you...while I watch." I could hear Con swallow carefully as he continued, "I want to watch you lick her out for me Bad Girl."

"Okay, that would be fine." I spoke as if confirming a dinner date as my final workmate brushed past my arm on her way out of the office. Following suit, the fresh air hitting my face with much needed refreshment, I fleetingly considered what he was actually asking of me, and what I'd automatically, unthinkingly agreed to.

"You really are my Bad Girl aren't you?"

"Oh, yes." I gripped the phone tighter. I had so many questions, but my throat had tightened, and my voice seemed to have got stuck on mute for the moment.

"Be at my place in one hour."

"An hour, I…" The line had gone dead. One hour! Only one hour to get ready! To get ready for an occasion I had no idea how to prepare for.

All thoughts of eating gone, I rushed home in record time. Feeling mildly sick with nervous apprehension, I threw my clothes off, jumped into the shower, thanking the god of dubious enterprises that I had shaved my legs the night before. Getting clean was easy, but what to put on once I was? And what if she hated me? What if I didn't fancy her? Already a picture of what she might be like was forming in my imagination.

I was pretty sure she'd be blonde. My lover might go for chestnut hair like mine in real life, but in fantasy land it would always be blondes he went for. Despite my fears I could feel my crotch twitching. The mere thought of Con watching me in action was enough to force me on. The fact he was going to watch me have a lesson in lesbian sex; well, the more I thought about it, the harder my nipples got, and it was a wrench to drag myself out of the shower, rather than wank myself off there and then beneath the jet of steaming water.

* * *

Fifty-five minutes later I was hovering on the doorstep of Con's small terraced home tucked away in the back streets of the city. Restraining myself from thinking too much, I had merely pulled on his favorite scarlet underwear, a miniskirt and blouse, before I ran from my flat. If I had begun to think too much, I would have chickened out and not made it there. Just like when the phone rang a month ago; I would never have let him bind me to a chair and reduce me to a begging, pleading wreck with two hours of silk cloth–related foreplay if I'd stopped to think. Or like when he met me in the back of a borrowed van and fucked me doggie-style in the middle of a busy street's turnout. Every vestige of my concentration had gone into not screaming and yelling out my climax and alerting the passing shoppers to what was happening behind the closed van doors.

Each time we meet I'm terrified, and each time I love every second.

My stomach churned as I knocked on the door, and my whole being felt vaguely dizzy.

Con opened the door, a massive self-satisfied beam across his face. "She's arrived." I nodded, too nervous to speak. This was as much to do with how I always feel when I'm with Con, as the lesson that I was about to take part in. There's something about the shine in his dark hazel eyes, the sheer confidence he radiates that leaves me in no doubt that we will have a good time. The fitness of his body; the aroma he gives off, not sweaty, not soapy, not horribly covered in masculine moisturizers, but unmistakably male. He stroked a rough hand down the front of my chest. "Scared Bad Girl?"

"A bit." My words were squeaky, and he laughed.

"And yet you'll love it won't you?"

"Yes." There was no other answer I could give him. I knew if he was there I'd love it. "What's she like?"

Con slipped a hand up beneath my miniskirt and firmly pressed his palm against my mound. I could feel myself quiver as my flesh reacted to the man who, after my years of a rather boring sexual routine with a meager handful of partners, had shown me just what my body could do. "You're wet already. What a slut."

My gaze met his, and I smiled. "Only for you. Your secret Bad Girl."

That was all he needed to hear, and the stiff shaft that had been digging through his jeans turned to rock against my thigh. Grabbing me by the wrist Con dragged me to his bedroom.

I almost tripped over my own feet as I was bought to an abrupt halt before the tall, mouth-wateringly curvaceous creature that stood before me. My suspicions had been correct: she was blonde, but natural, not the bottle yellow I'd been expecting. She was so relaxed, in total contrast to me: despite my extreme arousal, I was shivering more from uncertainty than desire. I suspect she was a professional, but I didn't ask. I didn't want to know.

Con shoved me toward his double bed and left me standing only inches from the female stranger, while he half sat, half lounged, on top of the laundry basket he kept in the corner of the room. His eyes glowed with a level of devilment that I'd not seen before. He didn't seem to blink as he stared at us, silent but expectant.

Still smiling, she took a step toward me and whispered in my ear, "I'm Tina. Are you ready for your lesson?"

Inclining my head a fraction, I felt a warm glow flooding my body as the other woman placed her hands upon my face. "Con tells me you kiss beautifully. May I?"

Again I nodded. Nothing had happened yet, but the world seemed to be spinning around me just from the pressure of her palms alone. When her ruby-painted lips met mine I melted into her. All I could think was, *Con's watching this. What's he thinking? Is he pleased? Are we turning him on?* My musings were answered with one long, deep guttural moan coming from the corner of the bedroom.

Once I was reassured that Con was happy, I began to relax into the kiss and allowed my arms to come to Tina's waist, my fingers hooking themselves into the band of her satin trousers. This was so different from what I was used to with Con. He was deliciously rough and forceful; Tina was gentle, exploring my mouth with her lips and tongue, and my back with her agile fingers. I could feel my breasts swelling under the cups of my lacy red bra and my confidence grew.

In my mind I could see pages from all those stories I'd read, all those paragraphs full of exotic erotic promise. Why had I imagined I wouldn't know what to do? I could picture every woman I'd ever read about being licked out, having her nipples pinched and massaged by female fingers, and I rapidly discovered that kissing wasn't enough for me.

Pulling away, I looked straight into Tina's blue eyes, and I knew she understood what I was thinking. She took my chin and bought my ear to her mouth, licking it softly before she whispered again, "You don't need teaching, but this is his fantasy you're living out, so we'll pretend. You want to give him a show."

It wasn't a question; it was a fact.

"He told me you were a bad girl." The gentleness faded, and she bit my neck with her brilliant white teeth, making me groan out loud, a groan that was again echoed by Con as he watched. "Well, so am I, honey."

Dragging me to the end of the bed, Tina pushed me so that

my back hit the duvet with a satisfying thump. In seconds my boots were off, my legs had been parted, my skirt was rucked around my waist and an active mouth was nipping and licking around my stocking tops. I reached my hands toward her head, but she slapped them away abruptly, saying sharply, "You will put your hands behind your head."

I didn't argue, placing my palms under my fast-knotting hair, as I willed her mouth to go higher, for my knickers to be yanked to my ankles, for more of everything.

Tina lifted her head, and I whined with loss as she addressed my lover, "Come closer, and I will show you what I am about to teach her."

All the time she spoke, her long slim fingers played with the top of my scarlet knickers. "A suitably colored garment for such a naughty girl, Con, don't you think?"

He growled his response, and as I turned my gaze toward him, I saw he'd lost his clothes; his skin was already blotched with the signs of excitement, and his shaft was indescribably hard. I wondered if he'd already started to wank before Tina called him over.

"Bad Girl!" I hastily returned my attention to Tina, who was playing the role of headmistress perfectly. Her stern hard tone turned me on further, returning me to the naughty submissive I need to be when I'm with Con. "You will close your eyes and pay attention to everything you feel. You will not—I repeat— you will not come."

Obeying, I sank back farther against the soft bed linen, my hand sweating lightly against my hair, as my enforced darkness heightened all my other senses. The sound of Con's breathing seemed to block out everything else; it was ragged and delib- erate, and I knew he was having trouble not spurting all over me there and then. I almost jumped off the bed when Tina's hands returned to me, ripping open my blouse so fast that at least one button pinged across the room. My bra was tugged beneath my tits, and the air started to caress them even before two hands sharply squeezed each nipple, sending painful hot darts of pleasure through my chest, directly to my clit.

Squeezing my eyelids tighter, I saws colors begin to gather as I reveled in every touch.

"In exactly two minutes"—Tina's voice seemed to be coming from far away as she continued to roughly pull at my tits—"I expect you to repeat all that is happening to you on my body. You will match these moves touch for touch, pace for pace. The more exact you are, the bigger your reward will be. After all"—her palms began to rotate over the very tips of my breasts, making it harder and harder to concentrate on what my pseudo-teacher was telling me—"you are here to learn, and I do think a system of praise for good work and punishment for poor work is the best way to educate, don't you, Bad Girl?"

There was no way I could answer. I was too wrapped up in the electric currents that ran between her fingers and my over-sensitive flesh as one hand broke away from my tits and began to stroke the strip of hair that protected my pussy. I tried hard to repeat the pattern of her routine in my head. Pinch nipples, rotate palms, move hand to mound…yet all the time I could hear Con's heavy breathing; I could smell his cock and feel the lust radiating off his body. His presence shot my concentration to pieces.

My shoulders began to ache, and I was desperate to move my hands, to bring them forward and grab Tina's chest; a chest I longed to see in the flesh. That was when the lesson really began.

"I hope you are paying close attention." Tina spoke sternly before her lips came to my pussy. My arse leapt forward as if it had been hotwired, and I couldn't help but lift my crotch toward her mouth. It was so familiar and yet somehow so different from the sensation of male lips between my legs.

As she moved her languid tongue, I tried to focus on each action. She drew it left, then right, and circled my clit with frustrating stealth. With my eyes firmly shut I couldn't see Con's face, but I was sure I knew how he'd look: intense, flushed and totally focused on the muscle that was sweeping across my nub with moist precision.

Grateful that I hadn't been prevented from making a noise, I mewled in satisfied bliss, my back arching again as Tina increased the speed of her laps. I longed to open my eyes, to see her, to watch Con as he observed me, hoping like hell that when it came to my turn to lick out the other woman, as per his fantasy, I wouldn't disappoint either of them.

My crotch began to twitch uncontrollably, and I braced myself for the first female-inspired climax of my life. A finger was now playing lightly at the entrance to my channel. I couldn't help but beg for Tina to slide it inside; that was all I would have needed to tip me over. For a second I thought she was going to do it, as a fingernail scratched itself carefully around the edge of my clit, but then abruptly, Tina withdrew.

The cry of loss I let out was engulfed in the long exhalation of air that shot from Con as he realized that the moment to see me orally stimulate a woman had arrived.

"Now." Tina stood up, appearing for all the world as if she'd been doing nothing more interesting than teaching me to spell. "Let's see if you are a model pupil or not."

With shaking legs, unable to believe I was supposed to do this whilst on the cusp of an orgasm, I opened my eyes and swapped places with my teacher.

Glancing at Con for reassurance, I was encouraged by his

demonic smile, and the stiffness of his cock that seemed to be telling me that I could do this, and that when I did, it would be the reward.

Flexing my fingers, getting the blood flowing again after their period of confinement beneath my head, I took a deep breath, and in as commanding a tone as I could muster, I told Tina to put her hands behind her golden head, and to spread her legs as wide as possible, I shoved her black skirt up and clumsily dragged her knickers down.

Repeating over and over in my head the pattern of what she had done to me, I placed my perspiring hands on her legs, and instructed her to close her eyes. Then, grabbing at the crisp white blouse she wore, I yanked at the buttons. Inhaling sharply at the sight of her braless tits, I paused. I knew I was supposed to be pinching the nipples, but I couldn't, not yet. Suddenly every girl-on-girl tale I'd ever read flashed through my mind, every literary touch, every imagined stroke of female flesh. I wanted to kiss the full firm globes that lay before me. I wanted to lick them, savor every inch of the areolas, kneel down and examine them at close range.

Con let out a deep whine, and I snapped back to the reality of the task I'd been given. Yet, I knew that somehow my hesitation was inflaming him more. In that split second, I decided not to stick to the plan, not to follow the pattern of Tina's movements, which I'd mostly forgotten the order of anyway. After all, I was supposed to be a bad girl.

Adopting an abrupt no-nonsense tone, I told Tina not to move or speak. "But that wasn't what I did to you?"

"I told you NOT to speak!"

Con looked at me in total amazement, and I swelled with pride as his smile turned into a beam and he took a step nearer, whispering, "That's my Bad Girl."

Tina's eyes flew open, and she turned to look at Con, who merely shrugged, "I told you she was very naughty. I suggest you do what she says."

Feeling as if I was on the outside of myself, looking down at a part of me I hadn't known existed, I set to work on her breasts, lapping, licking, nipping and kissing the porcelain skin with fervor. I wanted to do everything, but most of all I wanted to cram as much of the soft, pliant breasts into my mouth as possible, while my hands traveled across her entire body.

Clawing and tugging at her garments so they fell to the floor or against the bed, I touched, scratched and kissed every inch of her torso, thighs and legs, but pointedly ignored the enticing triangle between her legs.

My lover was so close to me I could feel his breath on the back of my neck as he shadowed every move I made. Tina was mewling low and steady as her hips rose and fell; her neck rocked from side to side. I knew she was close, and I knew that only experience was stopping her from pleading with me to touch her between her legs and let her come.

Con's huge hands gripped my shoulders, and his chest came up against my back as he pressed himself to me, his dick rubbing my legs. It was time.

Stamping down any lingering doubts about my ability to please another woman, I let go of Tina entirely, enjoying her howl of temporary bereavement, before I dropped to my knees, took a firm hold of her legs, and, with Con holding my ponytail away from my neck so he could see what I was doing, I took my first slow lap of pussy.

As the luscious moisture of her slick clit coated my tongue, I closed my eyes, recalling the movements that had crossed my own nub so recently. Burning with longing, I felt another climax gathering in the pit of my stomach as Con pressed himself harder against me, his body reeking of sex, his breath shallow.

Tina was quivering beneath me, and as my fingers snaked up to her nipples and squeezed them hard, she began to judder.

Con could wait no longer, and swiftly kneeling behind me, he tipped me so I was buried deeper into her crotch, before sliding himself into my soaking channel.

I don't know which of us came first as we bucked against each other, each calling out our own blissfully relieved satisfaction.

Con lay against the bed, one arm around my shoulder, the other snaked across my tits. "Are you sure you haven't done that before?"

Still high on my success at making two people come at once, I smiled happily, wondering what my work colleagues would say if they ever found out what their quiet accounting clerk got up to out of office hours. "Never, I just had erotic fiction and lust to fall back on!"

"Not to mention the fact that you are naturally a very bad girl." Con kissed my forehead with more tenderness than he'd ever shown me, before asking, "Fancy seeing Tina again? I have a plan."

"A plan?" Immediately my pulse quickened. "What plan?"

"You'll have to wait and see, Bad Girl, but I'm sure it won't be long before your phone rings again...."

DOLLY

Amelia Thornton

She was the prettiest dolly I had ever seen. Her skin was so white
and fragile, like it would shatter apart if I ever touched it, and her
eyes stared at me so beautifully vacantly, empty emeralds bored
into a porcelain shell. I wanted to brush her hair, feel the smooth-
ness of it running through my fingers, stroke the smooth sheet of
pure blackness hanging around her face like a dark curtain, put
ribbons in it and inhale the musty, rose-scented smell of it. Her
dress was a deep-green taffeta, with a pretty cream lace collar
and trim on the puffed sleeves and a wide black velvet sash tied
in an enormous bow on her back, and I wanted to take it off and
see what she looked like underneath, then put it back on and
take it off again, but I wasn't sure if she'd let me.

Dolly smiled a big smile at me. Maybe she was thinking I
looked like a pretty little girl too. I couldn't tell, because dollies
aren't really supposed to talk, and even though I wanted to ask
her, she probably wouldn't answer me. Daddy said I could have
whatever I wanted for my birthday though, and this was the

most super-duper-best-ever present he could ever get me, though where he found one as pretty as this I just don't know. I mean, I had mentioned it enough times, but I didn't think he'd really be able to find one. Not a real dolly, one who breathes and feels and suffers just like me; who I could play with, just me and her. But here she was, right in front of me, so smilingly silent. My perfect doll.

Gingerly, I stepped forward and poked Dolly's arm. She fidgeted a bit, but didn't move much. I poked her again. This time she kept completely still. *Hmm.* With an air of scientific experimentation, I took a large chunk of her beautiful black hair and gave it a good, hard tug. Her head lolled to the side, eyes still blankly staring ahead of her, enticingly unresponsive. I could feel an evil chuckle bubbling inside me as I pulled the other side of her hair, then the opposite one again, until her head was being mercilessly yanked from one side to the other. Dolly was going to have to get used to these kinds of games.

With all my might, I dragged her to the middle of the room and propped her up against the edge of the bed. That was the best thing about being a big girl on the outside, but a little one on the inside—you had all the strength of a grownup to pull a dolly around with, and considering Dolly was really quite a big girl herself, it certainly came in useful. I left her sitting like that for a bit whilst I got my very best tea set out of the cupboard, and I'm sure I saw her out of the corner of my eye twitch her head just a little to see what I was up to; but then every time I looked, she was completely still again. Damn sneaky for a dolly, that's all I can say.

With everything all ready and lined up, I crossed my legs on the floor and started to pour out some nice imaginary tea for Mr. Teddy and myself, and some for Dolly too of course, and I was perfectly content like that for a little while, chattering away to her and knowing she wouldn't dare to respond. I did start telling her about the time I tied up Mr. Teddy with my skipping rope to see if she'd get scared, but she didn't even blink an eye. She probably knew that Mr. Teddy was just a teddy, and wouldn't care two hoots if he got tied up or not, whereas the thought of tying her up was far more appealing. Maybe she was even hoping that I would do just that, and trying to goad me into it with her tempting little silences. Well, we would just see about that. Either way, I still couldn't stop thinking how I wanted to see what Dolly looked like under her dress, whether she would look like me, or like other girls; whether she would still be a dolly with her dress off, or whether she would magically become a girl again, like some kind of fairytale made real.

"Oh, whoops!" I suddenly said, very loudly, spilling my imaginary tea all over Dolly's dress. "Look at all that mess, Dolly! Daddy will be really angry if he sees you have a messy dress on. Do you know what happens to me when I make a mess?"

Dolly didn't say anything. She just kept staring straight ahead, smiling so very sweetly. *Hmm.* Maybe she knew it wasn't really a mess. That's the problem with dealing with a dolly who techni- cally speaking has all the cognitive facilities of a grown woman; she's going to know when you're making things up. I got up and scurried next door to the bathroom to fill my teapot with lots of warm water from the tap, and came back and stood right over Dolly, the teapot menacingly poised above her pretty little frock, and what I hoped was an evil glint in my eyes.

"You don't want to get in trouble, do you, Dolly?" I demanded. "You don't want to get taken over my knee and spanked black and blue for being such a messy girl, till I make you cry because it hurts so much, then cry a bit more? You don't want to have that happen now, do you?"

Still she said nothing. That was it. She deserved to be in trouble now. Slowly, so slowly, I tipped the teapot; I watched the water trickle slowly down her dress and across the shiny green bodice, slipping down to the skirt in watery snake-trails and forming a big, dark patch right on the front of it, sticking to her legs just a little bit. Maybe her skin would be wet underneath too. I wanted to touch it, feel the water soaked through the fabric to her smooth limbs, see if it felt cold or warm or just in between, see what she would do if my fingers slid past her petticoats and crept farther up and tried to... Dolly's arms flopped to her sides. She wasn't doing anything.

Firmly, I pulled Dolly up to her feet and sat myself down on the edge of the bed, yanking her roughly over my knee with every ounce of strength that I had. It felt good to be able to take charge like this, compelling and powerful and just so deliciously...moreish. It made me wonder why I didn't do it more, though I suppose I knew at the same time; it was the very same feeling she was probably feeling right then, that helpless, fathomless submission that comes from having another person take you over completely. I guess it's like eating nothing but cola cubes then having a jelly baby—both of them are yummy, so why have just one of them?

Sternly, I reminded myself I needed to be addressing the important tasks at hand, not just contemplating the relative merits of dominance and submission in terms of confectionary, and I tugged Dolly's limp torso a little farther over my lap so I could reach better. I did think I could see a flicker in her eyes, a tiny bit of fear, but then it was gone. Well, she'd be sorry soon enough. Daddy always takes his time when he smacks my bottom, over my dress, then over my panties, and then finally, very carefully, pulling my panties down; but I didn't have time for all that nonsense. Dolly's dress got pulled up right away, her pretty white lace knickers shoved down to her knees, and I smacked her as hard as I could, over and over and over. I know that's the very worst way you can spank someone, because I had it myself once, and it hurt like hell. No warming up, no gentle preamble, no time to get used to the sensation of someone's hand determinedly slapping against the softness of your skin. Just cold, hard ouch.

She was very good though, and didn't squeal or anything, not even when I got that awful spot right where the curve of her buttocks reached the top of her thighs. I did see her flinch a couple of times, and her feet kick out a little bit, but I guess even dollies can't help it sometimes. I could feel the water on her dress soaking through to my lap, a damp wetness spreading from her onto me, but I liked that feeling. It was just such a shame Dolly had to be punished for it.

It didn't take long for my hand to start to hurt, though. I don't know how Daddy manages it! Maybe you get used to it if you do it enough, and I suppose practice makes perfect and all that, but it wasn't really helping me in the current situation. So I decided to be resourceful, and pushed Dolly over to lie on her back on my bed while I went to find something else to teach her a lesson with, which couldn't be that hard in our house. Sometimes when me and Daddy aren't me and Daddy, but we're Master and slave, and Headmaster and schoolgirl, and other games Big Girls play when they're not being little, we have lots of nasty things to hit me with, but I wasn't too sure where Daddy kept them, and besides, little girls don't really have riding crops and cat-o'-nine-tails hanging round their bedrooms, and I do like to pay attention to details like that.

I did find my hairbrush, though. It's a beautiful hairbrush, all ebony wood and hand-plucked bristles, and Daddy told me it was very expensive and I'd better take good care of it. I did lose it once, but I was soon very sorry and had a very sore bottom and made sure I wasn't going to lose it again, not to mention having to use my pocket money to get a new one. That's the good thing about learning a lesson when you do something wrong; it focuses the mind so much more than just an average "don't do that again" ever could.

I glanced over at Dolly. She was still lying there, her eyes like glass, her long limbs stretched limply across my bluebell-print sheets, a silent little temptress. She looked like she deserved a good hairbrush spanking. Slowly, ever so slowly, I crept over to her, the mattress squeaking as I climbed up on the bed next to her and peered into her face. In the corners of her beautiful green eyes, I could see the beginnings of tears glistening. Poor Dolly. Gently I pulled her dress away from her long, pale legs and ran my fingers along her skin. It felt yielding and soft, not at all like porcelain. Maybe it wouldn't shatter after all. I gave it a good, hard pinch, just to be certain, and felt it surrender to me— clutched between my finger and thumb, coaxed into malleable submission. I liked the way that felt. I wondered momentarily if she would bruise, like I do, purplish blue dancing beneath her skin, fading to shadows of yellow as days passed. Dollies probably can't feel it like little girls can, I decided, and brought the hairbrush down with vicious force against the inside of her thigh, making her jump in shock, leaving a stinging red mark against her whiteness. It looked very pretty. Maybe dollies do get bruises after all. As I gazed with fascination at the fading blush of her skin, it made me want to make more marks on her, cover her pretty legs with angry redness, see what it would look like. So I did.

Each time I smacked the hard wood against her leg, her body would become rigid, and she would move, ever so slightly, with the force of it, then lie back, motionless, waiting for the next strike. Her eyes were becoming wild and desperate, pleading with me to stop, but her beautiful painted mouth remained silent, unable to form any words. How awful for her, to not be able to stop me, to just have to lie there and take it, pain twisting and whirling inside her head, to have to give over like this. I was so mesmerized by her inanimate limbs, her manic emerald eyes. She was ever such a good dolly, really. I would have been squirming all over the place if it had been me.

Still, I decided I didn't want to take any chances. I landed a particularly brutal final smack on poor Dolly's leg, watching with satisfaction as it burnt a furious red next to the criss-crossing random ovals I had already created, and hopped off the bed. I needed to find something to make sure she couldn't get away from me, could never leave her little girl and all these fun games we were having.... Now, where would Daddy have put it...? Aha! There it was. I wriggled myself underneath the bed, reached out my fingers and finally managed to grab the ends of a tightly wound pile of ropes. I was sure Dolly wouldn't try to play any tricks on me, but you never know. Better to be on the safe side with these things, especially when your dolly is big enough to overpower you, force you over her knee and dish out just the same punishment you've given her.

I scrambled to my feet and began neatly uncoiling them, taking hold of Dolly's wrists and wrapping the rope securely around them again and again, tying it firmly in a knot. I could feel the rough edges scratching at my fingertips, and thought how it must feel for Dolly to have it digging tightly into her hands like that, how helpless she must feel right now. It made me a little fidgety and excited to think about that. Carefully, I pulled Dolly's floppy body up so she was sitting, and began wrapping the ropes around her in pretty symmetrical patterns, pulling tight across all the parts that feel nice, admiring the shimmery green taffeta poking through the gaps in the rope and stroking where it cut into her soft arms. She looked so lovely all tied up like that, just waiting for me to decide what to do with her. So vulnerable: my little fairy-tale girl trapped inside her spellbound shell.

Finally, I took the last piece of rope and twisted it around her ankles, just to make extra sure she wasn't going anywhere, then pushed her up against the head of my bed so I could see her properly. She was looking quite a bit more disheveled now, her dress all scrunched up, her socks starting to fall down a little. She wasn't smiling so much either. Her panties were still tangled up around her knees, her legs a bright red mess of hair-brush-shaped welts, her torso squeezed tightly beneath twisting ropes. She looked even more beautiful now. I crawled over to her, watching her wince just a little, afraid of what I might do next, and I sat myself snugly on her lap, my legs straddling her helplessly bound body. It almost made me feel guilty for doing mean things to her. Almost.

Instead, I gently picked up my hairbrush and began to delicately run it through her tousled hair, smiling as I felt the tension in her body dissipate. It must be terrible, to not know what's coming next; to not know if I would make her smile slip even farther down her lovely face, puddling in smears of makeup teardrops on the tip of her chin, or if I would stop and do nice things to her instead. She deserved nice things now, I decided. Even if she might not later.

"There, there, little Dolly…" I murmured soothingly, admiring how her hair shone so prettily as I brushed it. "I won't hurt you anymore… You've been such a good little Dolly… So very, very good."

Tenderly, I stroked her pale cheek, cool and pliable beneath my touch. I was so near to her now I could smell the delicate rose scent of her hair, inhaling it, burying my face in the folds of blackness; it felt like she was swallowing me up like that, like her hair was wrapping around me and cocooning me in its comforting embrace. I let the hairbrush fall to my side, forgotten, as my fingers coaxed the tangles from it, bringing it to my lips and closing my eyes as the silky strands fell across my face. My body was pressed in so close to hers now, I could feel the knots of the ropes digging into my chest as I pushed myself ever closer, rubbing my cheek against hers, holding her face in my hands and lifting it toward mine, gazing at it with longing and curiosity.

Slowly, uncertainly, almost frozen with hesitation and shyness, I pressed my lips against her painted mouth. It was so strange; it felt like my breath was sucked into her, her coolness evaporating, like she was real and unreal and something else all at once; like the fairy godmother had come and given her life at last. She tasted like violet sweets and sugary tea, her syrup-like spit slipping across my tongue as I pushed deeper, feeling the sharp pearls of her teeth, the curve of the roof of her mouth. Her movement still surrendered to me, she gave in as my mouth possessed hers; her fragile limbs still trapped, so beautifully bound; so perfectly, motionlessly submissive.

Beneath me, my thighs still crushingly circled her bound torso, the handiwork of my ropes so alluringly abrasive between my legs that just grinding into her made my nerves short-circuit; like I could see little blue sparks darting off of us where our bodies met, except my eyes were closed and all I could see were colors. She seemed to understand this, my Dolly, as she pushed her body up harder against mine, not a sound slipping from her lips as I twisted and turned and squirmed upon her, her intoxicating closeness enough to fill me with such beautiful sensations I would just explode if they weren't released.

But I knew they would be. I knew if I kept doing this, they

would flood out of me like a dazzling flash of white light, dizzying and head spinning and soaringly beautiful, ripping through each of my nerve endings like I was some kind of giant electricity pylon. For those precious few moments, when I could feel myself climbing, when I could see the other side and knew I was on the precipice, when the warm glow emanating from within me started to spread outward; those were the moments I managed to pull my mouth away from hers enough to look into her perfect face and know that she could really, truly see me as it happened.

I wonder if she could feel my chest hammering against hers afterward. I think she probably could, since it felt like it was going to jump out of my throat and into hers. Kissing the lids of her emerald-green eyes, I pulled her closer to lie next to me, cocooned in my ropes, my arms entwined around her body. I knew there were many more games we had yet to play. Together, we slept in dreamless sleep and waited for Daddy to come home.

NO REST FOR THE WICKED

Jacqueline Applebee

Fear and desire have always meant the same thing to me. Roller coasters, scary movies and ghost stories all have the same effect. Fear turns me on.

Phillip was the boy next door. He was fourteen, four years older than me when his family moved in. Phillip was tall and surprisingly strong. I'd invite myself over and then proceed to make fun of the way he looked; goad him with cruel words just so he'd pay me the kind of attention I craved. That usually meant he would pick me up, and dangle me over the railing of the stairwell. I would always scream and laugh. He would always peek at my knickers as he held me by my legs, shaking me until I apologized. I loved it. I used to feel a fluttering as the beats of sensation traveled across my groin. My body used to feel funny 'down there' in a time before I had words for sexual arousal: dirty perv or happy little slut.

Phillip soon caught onto my games but he never took it personally. With the passing years my little body grew big and buxom. Philip and I played off and on, our adventures getting bolder as we grew older, but once I put on the extra weight, the dangling over the stairwell ended.

Philip and I remained good friends as adults; each of us had a mutual respect for the other's depravity. When my friend got engaged to a burlesque performer named Fanny Royale, I wished him all the best. I knew his wife-to-be would have a fine time with my naughty neighbor. I received an invite to their wedding a few months later, which is where I met Ken. As soon as I saw him I felt the familiar tingle over my labia. The wedding reception was held in a hotel on the Brighton coast. The happy couple celebrated with a disco that ran late into the night. I'd spent most of the evening flirting unsuccessfully with Fanny's bad-boy friends. I admired long arms decorated with tattoos, hard silver and steel in lips and brows. However, not one of them wanted to have a dance, share a drink or feel me up. It was nothing to lose sleep over, but I was pissed that they wouldn't at least give me a try.

Ken was different. He looked straight-laced, dressed as he was in a cream linen suit. Unlike most of the other men, Ken had no visible piercings and no tattoos on show either. His floppy brown hair was the only thing relaxed about him. He was the complete opposite of the kind of man I'd usually be attracted to. He moved slowly and gracefully like he was about to start a waltz. But his brown eyes never stopped moving, darting this way and that. Of course he made a beeline for the dance floor.

There was something about this man, something hidden that made the flutter intensify, like ice being rubbed across my nipples. I was intrigued to find out what it was about him that made me tingle with fear.

Ken, for his part, was unsure of me: a big woman radiating fuck-me-now vibes with every heave of my bosom. He sauntered over to me, keeping time to the music. He was intrigued too. A waitress scooted past with a tray of little cakes. Ken swiped two, passed one to me, and then licked his fingers. "Sweet."

I held the cake out at arm's length.

"Not hungry?" he asked. "You gotta love cake."

"I'm allergic to milk."

"That must be a pain." He looked a little embarrassed.

I shrugged, passed the cake back to him. "I can handle it."

"Does that mean if I kiss you, you'll go into shock?"

"You'd have to have a mouthful of cream for that to happen," I said with a wink.

Ken grinned at me. "Kinky." He ate the second cake in a few quick bites, and then he held out his hands, drawing me farther onto the dance floor. Standard wedding reception music played; power ballads and soft rock, but we danced anyway. The music suddenly changed just as I got into the rhythm. The tune that played was a fusion: old school jazz mixed with a techno beat. I latched on to the trumpets and clarinets and moved sensually, undulating like there was no one else in the room save for Ken and me. I felt his eyes on my body as he danced close, but not too close. His gaze traveled up and down though it kept returning to my breasts, trapped as they were in a laced-up bodice. I swung my big round arse an inch from his crotch. After a moment's hesitation he took hold of me; firm hands pulled me back so I could feel the solid mound that pulsed just like the track that played. We moved together, reckless, dancing like it was foreplay, although I received a couple of nasty looks from the skinny bridesmaids in their frilly dresses.

By the time the third tune ended, my dress was stuck to me in indecent places, but I was still hesitant to move away. I could feel Ken's sure hands with fingers that were certainly making an impression. It was time for me to take it further or stop and walk away.

Ken saved me any worry. "Let's get out of here." He was smooth and willing too, but I wondered if he really had the sharp flash of danger that I needed.

I led Ken up to my hotel room. I shut the door behind us, flicked on the small table lamp so we weren't in utter darkness. Ken swayed his shoulders; at first I thought he was dancing to the remnants of the tune that I could still hear playing if I strained my ears hard enough, but he was simply taking off his jacket. He turned, caught me looking at him. I grinned and started unlacing my top. That was when I felt the mood change. Ken was still, probably for the first time the whole evening.

"Problem?" I slipped the garment over my head and reached back to unhook my bra. Ken reached out a hand to stop me.

"You sure about this?" He gave me a long look. "You don't have to prove anything."

I gave him a sideways look. "You've never had a fat girl before have you?" I caught the rise of color that blossomed and then disappeared almost immediately. "There's just more to play with, that's all." I slid my arm around him trying not to sound desperate, but I was so horny I couldn't help myself. I circled him, pressed the swell of my belly to his back, danced around to his front. "What do you want to do, lover?" I drawled. "I saw you gazing at my tits all night." Ken's eyes dropped to my breasts. His dark hair flopped down. "Do you want to come on them?" He visibly swallowed at that. "You could push me to my knees, make me suck you off, and then you could decorate my skin with globs of your thick white come." I swept my hands to his crotch. It felt like a wedge of steel was stuck there. I smiled to myself as I continued. "Or do you want to pinch my nipples, make me cry and then beg you to soothe the pain with your spunk?" I unclipped my bra, held both hands above my head and swayed to and fro. "Like I said, there's plenty to play with if you want to be really naughty."

Ken took off his shirt, glaring at me the whole time. I saw an intricate tattoo that curled in a circle around his right nipple in a pattern of red, blue and black.

"Nice," I said, nodding to his chest. Ken crossed his arms looking self-conscious. "Does it signify anything?"

"Ancient history," he muttered.

"Oh, did you use to be a bad boy?"

"Yes," he whispered. "You wouldn't have liked me back then. I was a different person."

I laughed and hit him on the arm. "Silly, I love bad guys. Where's the thrill in being safe?"

I hardly had time to think before Ken's hand was on my shoulder. "Get on your knees." He pushed me down.

"Oh, I'm a lucky girl. You didn't even spank me first."

Ken froze with one hand on his fly. "Get up."

I stifled a laugh as I stood. Ken whipped off his belt and doubled it in his hand like a pro. I shimmied out of my skirt and knickers and then bent over the bed. *Sensation,* I thought. *Life is all about sensation. Make me feel present, make me feel alive. Make me feel something I can remember when you've long gone.*

The first crack sounded incredibly loud. It was swiftly followed by another and another. There was no warm-up, no gentle swats, just intense blows of his belt on my arse. It was fantastic.

"You've got a dirty mouth," Ken crooned. "But I'll put that to use later, just you wait and see."

I arched my bottom higher. "Promises, promises," I sang from the bed, but then I stopped as I felt his hand on the back of my neck. My clit screamed as the air diminished. I gasped and wriggled. Ken let me go.

"Why did you stop?"

"I don't want to kill you."

"You aren't going to kill me." I sighed with disappointment. Ken gaped at me. "What the hell are you on?"

I wanted to tell him that I was high on life, or some other new age shit, but I held his hand instead. I place his palm flat against my throat. "This feels good. This turns me on."

He said nothing as he pressed me to the bed again. His hand returned to the back of my neck. I felt a pressure, but not too much. His hold was restraining, not threatening. The other hand was also busy; he continued to use the belt to beat my arse hard. But after a while that wasn't enough. Ken used his bare hands. I appreciated the difference between cold animal hide and warm human flesh. I could feel the sting where five tips of his fingers had made their mark. It's not often that I enjoy being a voyeur, but at that moment, I'd have done anything just to see his hand-print, a scarlet shade on my pale flesh. I'd have loved to see how my ample bottom jiggled with every spank delivered. My face pressed into the mattress instead. My hips bucked up, wanting more, wanting him. My wish was granted when I felt Ken's fingers press into my cunt that was hot, sticky and hungry. My internal muscles squeezed and clenched around the invasion.

"I ought to just shove my whole hand inside you," he said with a snarl in his voice. "You'd scream then, wouldn't you?"

I struggled beneath his hold, nodding my head fractionally.

"You think you're so bad. But I'm gonna show you."

The hand on my neck was suddenly gone. He twisted me around so that I lay facing him. Ken gave me just a second to gasp in a breath before he knelt over my wide hips. I was aware of the solid weight of him. I could not move an inch.

"When was the last time you did sit-ups?" he asked with a grin. His cock was free, pointing straight at me. I eased myself up with difficulty to plant a kiss to the head of his cock, relishing the salty goodness that collected at the tip. "This isn't going to work." He climbed off me, but in a flash, he dragged me off the bed to kneel on the floor. I felt Ken's hand as he gripped the ends of my curly brown hair, pulling my head back. A slice of pain shot through me. My mouth opened without a second thought. Ken stifled my cries with his cock, pushing it all the way in on the first go. I gagged around it for a few seconds, and then I welcomed that bad boy home. I wasn't blowing him, I didn't get a chance to use any technique, but I let myself be face-fucked until my lips burned, my tongue ached and I was ecstatic with pleasure. Ken slammed his hips against me, his cock deep inside my mouth. We both held ourselves still as he came. I gulped him down. He tasted wonderful.

I grinned at him, satisfied with what we'd done. "You see— you shouldn't be afraid of your bad-boy side. I had a good time." I wiped my sore mouth with the corner of the bedsheets.

"That wasn't my bad side." He yanked me up roughly. "You haven't seen my bad side, baby. But it's coming." Ken kissed me, tasting his own spunk as our tongues met. I looked into dilated eyes that still twinkled with naughtiness. "Don't even think I'm done with you." He shoved me down to sit on the edge of the bed. He fumbled on the floor, rummaging around in his jacket pocket. To my surprise, he produced a small knife. It was a little thing that could easily be mistaken for a comb in the right light. Ken squeezed my big tits together. "I seem to remember you saying something about these." I held my body still as he ran the flat of the blade over my left nipple and then my right. The cold tingle of the metal traveled straight down to my cunt. I was aware that my breathing had almost stopped. I was dripping wet, hungry for more sensation than I could bear.

Ken squashed both my breasts together so that my nipples

were almost touching. "Wow," he said with awe. "You can't do this with skinny girls." His mouth returned to my tits, biting and sucking me hard. "You really are more than a handful aren't you?" In a sudden movement he placed the knife to my throat. Time stopped dead. The room disappeared. My world only held two things: the glint of the blade and the hard constant pulse of my clit. I felt the press of metal beneath my chin, and with that I started to come. My movements were restrained by the threat of blood, but nothing could hold back the orgasm that tore through me. Ken paused, watched me quake, and then continued to swirl the knife all over with just enough pressure to scratch, but not enough to pierce my skin. I felt as if he were painting a portrait on my body with the deadly tip. The light in my hotel room must have been perfect, or maybe it was my orgasm that affected my vision, because that knife looked as big as a machete. Just the thought of it made my breath escape in one slow stream as I finally came back down to earth. When the blade returned to my throat once more it was no longer cold and lethal. The knife felt like a part of him. It felt good.

Ken dropped the blade and held me tight in his arms. We kissed. I had no air in my lungs, but somehow I was still alive, gripping him equally hard. Finally our mouths popped apart. I collapsed back on to the bed, gasping. I could suddenly hear music from the disco again, loud in my ears.

"That was intense," I murmured sleepily. "I was petrified."

Ken looked at me for a long moment before speaking. "You want to know something really weird?" he asked. I nodded once. "I get petrified of stuff too, but it doesn't turn me on. It just makes me want to run like hell." I held my arms open to him. He curled up beside me. "I guess I'm just a poor soul who's scared of intimacy."

"Don't bullshit me." I hit him weakly. "You're a bloody liar."

Ken started shaking with laughter. "You can't blame a guy for trying, can you?" He nipped at my earlobe, sparking a little thrill. "I'd hate for this to be a once-only event. And you'd get tired of my bad-boy persona eventually."

"Never. As long as you don't use a line like that again, you're welcome in my bed anytime."

Ken's smile was radiant. "I'd like that." He snuggled against my breasts, kissed along the lines and swirls he'd made. In time his kisses turned to bites. I felt the tingle return, chasing my drowsiness away. I ran my fingernails over Ken's shoulder, smiling as I listened to him hiss. It was going to be a long night, but my bad boy was definitely worth losing sleep over.

THE SKIN DOCTOR

Tsaurah Litzky

One morning I wake up and the little mole on my lower back is itching. It itches all day and that night it itches so much I have trouble sleeping. The next day it itches even more. I call up the skin doctor and make an appointment for the following week. A decent independent press has just published my poetry book to great reviews. How foolish, how futile it would be to be carried away by something smaller than a birth control pill, now that I may be entering the big time, now that I may be nominated for the Pulitzer Prize.

The day of my appointment with the dermatologist arrives and the itch in the mole on my back is acting like a fickle lover; it comes and goes. As I start to dress, I take great care choosing my panties because I know they are all I will be wearing during the examination. I am eager to see this skin doctor; I have seen him before and he is a very hot skin doctor. He looks like a man of experience, like Clark Gable in *The Misfits,* with the same little moustache above his upper lip, the same solid build and strong powerful haunches. I imagine that little moustache tickling my clit, as he teases it with a practiced tongue.

During my last visit, the skin doctor lifted and cupped my left breast gently with one hand while he used his other hand to deftly cut out a mole on my rib cage. His hand lingered, his fingers pressing my breast a few moments more than necessary.

"How are we doing?" he said with a sweet little squeeze as he let go.

I pull on my new, pink silk, French-cut panties. I stole them from Lord & Taylor a month ago because it excites me sexually to steal. I have a drawer full of purloined panties and I only steal from the best stores. All the way home on the subway I was so wet I wondered if the other passengers could smell me. I can see myself pirouetting in front of the skin doctor naked except for the panties. I know I won't be able to stop myself from blushing and creaming just a little bit on the fresh satin crotch. I wonder how much of my eagerness to see the sexy dermatologist has to do with the fact that I haven't gotten laid for six months.

The dermatologist's office is crowded. I sit on a brown leather chair and take my poetry book, which I carry with me everywhere, out of my purse. I make a show of opening it; hold it in front of me, pretending to read.

I hope someone will get curious about the beautiful cover and ask about it, but no one seems to notice. The skinny matron sitting across from me appears occupied by her own concerns. She chews her lower lip, twists her gold wedding band round and round on her finger. I wonder if she is worried about an errant husband or maybe she is nervous because she has forgotten to wear any panties under her floral print dress. I imagine her pale pudendum is hairless, surprisingly rosy and plump.

Next to her sits a teen boy with a bad case of acne. He is staring into her lap; maybe he has X-ray vision and is fascinated by her bald cooch. I decide that under his baggy pants he has a slinky purple cock that looks like a gecko lizard. I wonder if his lizard cock will creep down the leg of his pants, crawl up over the arm of his chair toward her and then dart down under her skirt and up between her thighs. Perhaps she will leap to her feet, screaming, or maybe she will just sit still and enjoy it. That's what I would do. I'm so starved for cock.

Just then a nurse comes into the waiting room and calls my name.

I follow her into an ultramodern examining room. The steel instruments arranged in trays on the cabinet are polished, gleaming. The walls are so stark and white they hurt my eyes. I put my backpack on the floor and I perch on a stool with a plastic seat. I open my book, which is still in my hand. I want to impress the dermatologist with my book just as I want him to like my body in my pink panties.

I am reading the "Vagina Blessing Poem"—*celebrate the words for vagina that are supposed to be dirty but are not… cunt, clit, pussy, hole, snatch twat*—when the door opens and the skin doctor steps into the room.

"Hello," he says, "it's been a while," and he extends his fine, large hand. The moustache seems fuller, bushier. He is even more handsome then I remembered. Once he told me he was born in Marseilles, and he has a faint French accent. I put my hand in his and he raises my fingers to his lips. His glance falls on my book.

"What is this?" he asks. "What are you reading?" I try not to simper as I answer, "It's my book, my new poetry book."

"Congratulations. Let me see," he says. He reaches down and grabs the book out of my hand. His gaze focuses on the open page. I see his brow furrow and the corners of his mouth turn down as he reads.

He sighs, "Writing about one's private parts and in the most explicit language is very popular nowadays," he says, and he shakes his head. "You must write like this because you want to sell books." I can't believe it; can this man who has seen thousands of tits and thighs and asscracks actually be a prude? I feel my temperature rising. What does he think skin is for anyhow?

"Sex is part of being human; it's nothing to be ashamed of," I hear myself say defiantly. "It's nature." He does not reply, instead he thrusts the book back into my hand. I put it back in my backpack as if protecting it from him.

"Now," he asks sternly. "What is on your mind?" I want to say, I was having a fantasy about wanting to fuck you, but you're too square for me. Instead I tell him about the mole.

"Let's have a look," he says. "Take off all your things except your panties." He drags the word panties out, giving it an ominous sound like hysterectomy. "And put on the surgical gown behind you on the examining table." He leaves the room, slamming the door.

This unpleasant exchange has made me feel sad and rejected. I want to dash from the examining room back out to my beloved, New York summer streets. I'll run across Tenth Street to Broadway, then down Broadway to the Brooklyn Bridge and walk across. The view from the bridge, the sight of the graceful river below and the Statue of Liberty, will lift my spirits. Then the mole on my back starts to itch again; it reminds me how important it is that I take care of myself.

I strip except for my lovely pink panties, which now look silly and cheap. I place my clothes on the stool, don the surgical gown and perch on the corner of the examining table. I wrap my arms around my chest and hug myself. It's cold in the room, so cold; maybe I should get up and light a fire like in that Jack London story, or I'll freeze to death. I can use my book for kindling—but suddenly I have no energy. I hug myself tighter, close my eyes. I'm very tired; I feel like I'm falling asleep.

A warm breeze wakes me and I hear the door open and shut. I open my eyes to see the skin doctor standing above me. He has put on a pair of thick glasses and is now wearing surgical gloves.

"Turn your back to me and take off your gown," he says. "I'll look at that little mole you're talking about, then check your other beauty marks and moles."

I follow his instructions and then I hear him stepping up behind me. "So this is it," he says and I feel the cool rubber of his fingers tapping the mole. "Any pain now?" he asks. "No," I say, "not at all." I feel him kneading and pulling the skin beneath his fingers "How about this, any pain?" he queries. "Nothing," I answer.

He steps even closer, and I feel something warm and wet in the middle of my back. It's his tongue! He is tonguing my skin! His tongue finds my mole, presses against it.

"What about this, any discomfort now?" he whispers. I am too shocked to say anything as his tongue continues to progress down my spine. Slowly it teases its way beneath the elastic of my panties. It feels delicious, but aren't there rules about this? Should I turn around, yell, *Wait a minute, what are you doing?* This is not professional, but I like what he is doing too much and I already feel a warmth, a loosening between my legs.

Maybe he can read my mind, because he gives me a chance to protest. He stops his tonguing long enough to say, "Tell me, are you at all uncomfortable? Shall I continue?" I take a giant step across the chasm of fear and loneliness that has encircled my life for far too long. My skin needs skin and I want it. I want it now!

"No," I say faintly and then more firmly, "No, I'm not uncomfortable at all."

He whispers into the small of my back, "Well, then," and his tongue slips beneath my panties again. He uses it to caress the bottom of my spine, finds my Kundalini spot. He kisses there; he sucks with a hot, moist mouth and a blissful wave of heat spreads all the way up my spine and out through my body. My nipples perk up, my clit swells with longing.

His wily tongue strikes out for territory farther south. It slides into my asscrack with a sleek kissing sound. The tight little bud there opens; he has found out my secret pleasure as he diddles me with his slick tongue. In and out, in and out it goes. His rhythm is so steady and practiced I wonder if this is part of the curriculum in dermatology school. His fingers on my buttcheeks pull them wider so his tongue goes deeper and deeper within. My pelvis starts to move. I know I can come like this but then he stops and pulls his magic tongue out. He steps back, leaving my anus hungry and open and me dangling on the sharp edge of desire.

"We must not hurry the examination," he says. "It is important to be thorough. Are you all right?" he asks. I manage to gasp out, "Fine." My panties have fallen to my ankles. "Now step out of your panties," he instructs me. I do and then, "Turn around," he says.

The first thing I notice is that his glasses are all fogged up. He takes them off. He picks up my panties from the floor and sniffs the crotch. "Ah, Chanel Number Five," he says with a little smile. Then he polishes his glasses with my panties and puts the glasses back on. I am so excited that my breath is coming in little puffs like the locomotive of a toy train.

"I see no irregularity so far," he says, "but there is still a spot that must be examined, one quite difficult to reach. For this, I will have to use a special instrument."

He unbuttons the lower button of his white coat and lifts it high. He undoes the buckle of his belt and pulls it off. His unzips his fly and inserts his hand to pull out a thick, red cock coiled like a rope. He pulls his huge red balls out too. The cock uncurls in front of me; points right to my heart of hearts.

He takes a step closer. "Sometimes it is necessary to examine the breast orally," he says, and he bends his face and sucks my nipple into his mouth. He nurses with vigor, sucks me roughly just the way I like it, while his cock keeps brushing against my leg. I can't stop myself from pushing closer to him, grinding my pelvis against his, the long lariat of his cock pressed between us.

He steps back, releasing my nipple. "Stay calm, *ma petite,*" he cautions. He lifts me and sits me down on the examining table.

"Now," he says, "I prepare my instrument." He opens a drawer in one of the cabinets along the wall. He takes out a long transparent rubber tube that he pulls onto his cock. He steps closer, "Now, turn over and get on your hands and knees with your bottom facing me" he says. "You are a literate woman," he says. "I am sure you know this is called doggie position. Now, lift your bottom up and spread your knees."

He slips a hand between my legs and pulls open my nether lips.

"*Bien, bien,*" he murmurs. He slips his fingers into me, testing my heat, "You are ready, very ready." He pulls his fingers out and then I feel his tool slowly probing inside me, expanding into every crevice as he moves deeper into my flesh. I find myself embracing his miraculous instrument with my whole body, pulling him into my center. He moves faster, his heavy balls spanking my bottom. I start to come, moving my hips so with such vigor I hit him in the chin with my ass. This seems to excite him even move. He grabs my hips to hold me steady and as he pounds into me we climax together.

"*Merci, merci,*" he cries out as he comes. He falls onto my body. I feel his moustache tickle me then he gently bites my shoulder and kisses my neck. I am exhausted but so happy and I'm not itching anywhere. I close my eyes. I'm dozing, falling into a dream.

I am on the stage in a big, crowded auditorium. Rows and rows of expectant faces look up at me. The dermatologist is seated in the front row gazing at me adoringly. I am reading from my book, from the "Vagina Blessing Poem." I finish to tumultuous applause. The applause grows louder and louder; the audience stands up clapping, whistling, cheering. The noise is deafening. I open my eyes to find myself staring at the pristine white ceiling of the examining room, the glaring, fluorescent light. I am alone. What I hear is not applause, but a loud insistent knocking, the sound of a fist on wood.

"Are you ready in there yet?" the skin doctor calls though the door. "Hurry, please, I have other patients waiting."

I pull myself up into a sitting position. The gown is still tied tight around me. "I'm ready now," I say.

PAGODA

Sommer Marsden

"It's a full moon," Bruce tells me.

Before I can fully process the words, a shiver runs up my back like some small invisible creature planting little footprints of anticipation along the track of my spine. My only answer is, "Tonight?"

"If it doesn't rain." He gets in the shower and leaves me to suffer.

The skies all day are pregnant with potential rainfall. They hover close—low over us in varying shades of gunmetal gray. I have never wished so hard for clear skies and dry ground.

In fall the twilight settles down like a hastily thrown wool blanket. One moment the sky is dusky with nightfall the next it is full-on dark: a shroud suddenly tossed over the world.

"Time to go. You lucked out, Maisy."

I'm just thankful the moon is there for our full-moon tradition. We walk there. It's that close. It's only blocks to the garishly painted yellow and red pagoda a few streets over. In our neighborhood the small structure stands out like a grand building in the midst of a trailer park. It just doesn't make sense, and that's why the viewer is instinctively drawn to it.

Bruce was to do a piece for the local paper on oddities in local neighborhoods. That's how we found it. A pagoda built in what used to be someone's back yard, but what is now the back yard to a small neighborhood store. Funny thing is, no one knew the story of it or how it came to be, but the store owner let us take pictures.

"I want to splay you out on that concrete pad and fuck you," Bruce had said in my ear, while finding a good angle for his camera.

I'd shuddered and I'd blushed and my panties had gone so fucking wet in an instant. I hadn't known what to say so I'd said nothing.

"Maybe I'd tie you to one of the support beams; see how they're all scrollwork? Tie you there and let a crowd gather and just slip into you and put on a show under the plump full moon we'll have tonight. Maybe make you beg. Make you do something you'd never normally do—fuck in public. Maybe make you cry. I think people would like to see you beg and cry in a bright red and yellow pagoda."

He'd squatted down for an upshot with his fancy camera and I'd had no air. No words. Just a stunned and hotly flushed look on my face. At the last second he'd turned his lens to me and shot that expression.

That shot hangs on the wall in the foyer now. It is the one picture in which I think I look beautiful.

We'd gone back that night. He'd kept his whispered promises.

"It's chilly, yeah?" he says, pulling me into him, and I shake off my reverie. I touch one scrolled support for the pagoda.

"Yeah." I'm shaking.

Bruce tugs me harder and I study him from the corner of my eye. His head is shorn close and the stubble that has sprouted there is silver and chocolate. He's seven years my senior and he makes me feel both strong and vulnerable—a walking oxymoron.

It's one of the things I love about us.

We circle the garish structure, making sure no spotlights from the stores shine on it; there's nothing but moonlight; nothing but the stars. It's really bizarre how it sits out here in the middle of the bustle and hiss of the city as if it's on some serene mountaintop. The air is cool with a bitter cold undertone and it bites at my ankles, my nose, my fingers.

Bruce leans in, touches my nipple through my shirt. It pebbles from the outside temperature; it pebbles from his touch. This is my body's reaction to all that's going on around me and inside me—the cold, his intentions, my anticipation, the feelings so thick like syrup clouding my thoughts.

"Take your clothes off, Maisy," Bruce orders conversationally.

So I do.

I kick off my sliver-buckled flats, strip off my skinny jeans after unzipping the zippers at my ankles. I wear no panties under it all and he drops to his knees to place a kiss on each hip bone, his breath hot and welcome on my sex. I tug off my hoodie, my long-sleeved tee in the calming shade of lavender—though I feel anything but calm—and my bra is last. I stand in the pagoda completely bare and I shiver more from pleasure than from cold.

"Turn for me."

I turn and the darkness settles over my eyes, blacking out my sight with a soft kiss of satin. The sleep mask is what I always wait for. The mask that makes this all so illicit, so wanted, so coveted.

"Sit."

I drop to the cold concrete pad that is the floor of the structure. I sit and I wait and I try so hard to hear my ears ring. After a while, I hear a shuffle to my left, a scuff to my right. I hear my own wildly racing heart and my own short, stunted breaths. I hear distant traffic and the call of some night bird. I hear more whispers of steps and remind myself, it could actually be others. Or it could just be Bruce walking in brisk circles around the pagoda to mess me up. I simply don't know.

But then I hear a zipper and he's close. I can feel him like an electric current running over my skin. My flesh is a rash of goose bumps: from the cold, from adrenaline.

"Open your mouth for me, Maisy. Make room for daddy," Bruce says and laughs softly. His voice, though normal volume, is big and booming to my ears thanks to my blindness.

I part my lips and feel the silken press of his cock to my bottom lip. It's soft and velvety and impossibly warm. My tongue snakes out, gathering the salty drop of precome I know will be there. My heart is beating so hard I feel almost sick and my pussy is a flood of warmth even in the cold fall air. Is someone there besides us? Is there a crowd? Is it just us?

I have no way of knowing. He won't tell.

Sometimes I hear soft secretive sounds, but your ears play tricks on you when the world is dark. Perception is a mysterious thing.

I smell cigarette smoke but can't tell if it is far away or up close. The wind whips it up and around in the frigid air so it is impossible to tell. And all the while my mind struggles so hard to focus, my body is humming in unison with its activities. I suck Bruce's cock and he cups my head with his big warm hands as he buries himself deep in my throat. He holds his hands half over my ears and that makes it harder to gauge sound and distance. All I can hear for true is his voice; all I can feel perfectly is the touch of his hands, trapping wisps of sound against the curves of my ears.

"I could come right like this," he says, his accent thickening with his arousal. He's from New England and when he gets excited you can cut it with a knife. "But I don't think I will. I don't think I will at all."

He pulls free of me and I hear a sigh. Is it him, is it me, is it someone else? That is the question after all. He pushes me back with a boot to my shoulder. It's not a rough action, just decisive, and I fold myself back, lay myself flat—feel the prod of his work boot to my hip bone. He rests the rugged sole on my pelvis and my heartbeat is trapped in the cage of my belly for a moment, thumping with a primal beat. Bruce toes my thighs apart and I can feel him standing over me.

I hear the whisper of skin on skin, like hand on cock, and I wonder, is it him or a watcher? My nipples grow impossibly hard, almost painfully so. A finger touches one stiff tip, strokes it, and I feel my eyes prick with tears behind my mask. My pussy flexes with wet expectation and I say just, "Bruce, oh, Bruce..."

"Say *please*."

"Please."

"Say *baby*."

"Baby, please," I say.

He drops over me then. I feel the rugged denim kiss of his jeans on the inside of my thighs. I feel the brush of his warm hard cock to my cunt opening, the flicker of my sex flexing to take him, the heady rush of my own fluids to aid his way and when he slips into me there is a whisper-sigh-shuffle to my left, my right, behind me and I wonder, wind or watchers?

I grasp my legs around his hips, taking him deep as his sharp teeth trap my pulse at my throat. He leaves his teeth there as he thrusts, fucking me hard so my lower back is scraped and ripped along the rough pavement. His breath fills my head, a ragged animal sound as he ruts and fucks and scoots us along the moon-dappled concrete that I can only see in my mind's eye.

I imagine them there: the leering, the curious, the horny, the sad. Couples touching each other, lonely men touching themselves, young men and old men. Women who just want to see. Those who have stumbled upon us by accident. The lonesome and the nosy and the perverse. Watching us with avid eyes as we fuck in the pagoda, shot through with the light from a fat, silver moon.

My cunt clutches up around him, my fingers pluck at his warm flannel shirt. I let him bury his tongue in my mouth and I kiss him back like it might be my last kiss. The orgasm uncurls and plucks me down with thin, hot fingers of lust and pleasure. I fall backward into it, the earth dropping out from under me, or so it feels. Bruce pushes his lips to my ear. His stubble snags my hair. He bites my lobe before he whispers.

"Maisy, my beautiful Maisy. Rhymes with daisy, never lazy, come for me again."

It is a nonsense thing he says to me. It is a comforting little rhyme. But he follows it with a sharp nip of his teeth and his fingers have found my nipple again and pinch and he thrusts once more hard and I obey, coming for him again.

He traps my hands at my sides, denying me the sense of touch. I'm blind, I'm trapped; I feel his racing heart and his heavy breath and he stutters over me in a chaotic, frantic way that says he's no more good. His cock thrusting deep inside as my body lets off little ticks and blips of pleasure from my orgasm. I grip my muscles tight to feel him perfectly and that is that. Bruce roars in my ear, his voice like the ocean as he comes. His whole big body drops down flush on mine so that the air rushes out of me and small white dots dance in my vision under the eye mask I wear.

He says in my ear, "Stay."

He gets up and I lie there, shaking with a palsy caused by cold and nerves. My own wetness mixed with his is spilling out of me. There I am, bare and naked and splayed—something dirty and beautiful, used and cherished. I lie there as I hear footsteps and claps, sighs and whispers, coughs and movement.

The kicker is, they could all be Bruce. A trick of sound and motion and air and wind. His deliberate mind game with me because he knows how much I crave the feared and wanted exhibitionism. It could be just him...or it could be a whole cluster of others, watching and judging our fucking. I'll never ever know. Bruce always makes me keep the blindfold on until we're all done. It's possible that sometimes we are observed and others we are not.

I'll never know.

After what seems like a million years but isn't, he says, "Okay," and I feel him drop the warm bundle of my clothes into my lap.

I pull the mask off and he helps me up, kissing me hard, pulling me in to hold me and then helping me dress. The chill has seeped into my bones and wormed into my muscles and I am shaking hard. Bruce pulls off his flannel and bundles me in it. We walk home slowly, hand in hand.

"I'm going to fuck you again when we get home," he says. It's a lazy, softly spoken statement. Not a question.

I nod and smile and feel that tremble in my belly that says I want him again. I want him more than heat or blankets or a hot shower.

"Just me and you this time."

He says it with a secret smile. I smile back. Because I know—or think I do in that instant—that it's probably all just been him. All the little sounds when we visit the pagoda. It's simply him walking around me, whispering, toying with me and playing up acoustics and imagination. Or maybe it's not...

I'll never know.

That's the whole point.

A WIDER WORLD

Donna George Storey

For one dizzy moment I wonder if it's a trick of the lamplight or a vision born of the citrus-spiked glow of the Grand Marnier. Maybe it's simply auto-asphyxiation, because I've been sitting here holding my breath for a full minute.

I blink twice and take a gulp of air.

No, this is absolutely real.

A man I met just a few hours ago is about to undress his wife before my eyes.

And we—my husband and I—are going to stay and watch it happen.

The scene of this debauchery *à quatre* is the lovely home of Rick and Sara Porter, a spacious California ranch house with tasteful furnishings and original art on the walls. Paul and I are cradled in the sumptuous cushions of a module sofa, our shoulders and hips pressed together, no doubt to keep each other from falling over at the sheer audacity of what we're doing. Rick and Sara sit on an identical sofa positioned directly across the glass coffee table. For an hour we've been the mirror image of each other, two oh-so-worldly couples in our thirties doing our best to be witty and charming. But now Sara is lying back in her husband's arms while he undoes her silk blouse slowly, as if the sensation of each button slipping from its prison gives him unspeakable pleasure.

I've always been polyamorous at heart. I firmly believe the erotic urge thrives on freedom and variety. Lock it up under the care of a single jailor, and it wastes away to nothing.

My eyes are glued to Rick's thick fingers as they work their way down the ladder of pearl buttons. My own fingers begin to throb. I grip my thighs to steady myself.

Rick gives his wife a secret smile, then eases the blouse over her shoulders. Sara's breasts are generous, barely contained by a bra of a sparkling translucent material. Was it chosen in the hope we might see it? Immediately my eyes are drawn to her dainty pink nipples poking up through the thin fabric. I feel my own nipples chafing against my bra, a black satin push-up. As much as I tell myself I'm the corrupted innocent, I, too, have dressed for a night of possibility.

Sara shimmies out of the blouse, and Rick drops it on the carpet with a magician's flourish. He pulls her back into his embrace, stroking her upper arms with his fingertips. The pressure of his hands serves to accentuate her cleavage, framed by the glittering lingerie. Even her flesh seems to shimmer.

My husband exhales audibly and shifts in his seat.

Still we both keep staring.

I've always been an exhibitionist. By which I mean I get turned on watching others get excited by watching me.

Sara's eyes swoop languidly from Paul to me and back again. She is clearly enjoying what this is doing to us. I'm sure she sees my cheeks blushing brick red, my chest rising and falling in quick gasps. Paul has grown a lump in his khakis so big you could spot it from a mile away.

Rick unsnaps Sara's bra with a faint click. It sags over her chest, momentarily shielding those proud nipples from view. He pulls the straps down over her arms and pauses devilishly. She twists against him and purrs, "Please." With a quiet laugh, he slides the bra over her arms and tosses it on top of the blouse. Sara arches her back. Her breasts hang full and heavy from her slender rib cage.

I've always been a show-off in my daydreams. But I didn't realize how deep my desire ran until one night when we were on vacation in Maui. We'd met a couple at the resort where we were staying. There was something about them that intrigued me, a special sparkle in their eyes. They invited us to their bungalow for drinks, and after a few, the husband dared me to share a sexual fantasy. I can never resist a dare.

Rick cups his wife's breasts in his large hands. His thumbs find her nipples and flick them knowingly. She tilts her head back, baring a smooth throat.

Trapped in their satin harness, my own breasts tingle, jealous of her freedom. Jealousy creates false boundaries. That's what it said in a book Paul and I read about couples who "expand their horizons" with other partners.

I bought the book expecting to use it for nothing more than another of our private spouse-swapping fantasies in our safe little marital bed. But a few weeks later Paul met Rick, the CTO of a mobile banking application company, at one of the after parties at MacWorld. Paul was going to show him a clever app on his iPhone, when Rick admired his screen saver, a picture of me in a swimsuit. He happened to have a photo of his own fetching spouse on his phone. Maybe because he'd had a few beers, Paul made a joke about sharing in real life. When Rick replied that he and his wife—Sara ("no *h*")—occasionally enjoyed intimacies with other couples as a way to spice up their relationship, Paul's jaw almost dropped to the floor.

"It's obviously a sign from the universe," my husband told me when he got home from the party. "And we don't necessarily have to do anything sexual with them. Our first meeting would be more like an informational interview—like reading a book that talks back."

Neither of us was expecting how Sara would enchant us with mere words.

I told our inquisitive friend the first thing that came into my head. About how I've always fantasized that my lover would undress me for an appreciative audience and give them a demonstration of what turned me on, step by step. You should have seen his face—I swear he popped a boner on the spot. I thought his wife might be upset, but she's the one who said, "Why don't you do it right now? We're a very appreciative audience."

Sara is clearly aroused beyond speech now. Rick's right hand continues tweaking her nipple, while his left travels down over her belly and nestles between her legs. She pushes up against it to the rhythm of her own musical moans.

I squeeze my husband's hand. His wedding ring presses into my flesh.

"I'd offer to show them how wet your pussy is, but we don't want to push them past their comfort zone." Rick speaks in a half whisper, but we are obviously meant to hear.

"Uh, we're quite comfortable actually," Paul blurts out.

Rick and Sara laugh, and even I have to smile. I don't mind him speaking for me. I want to see her pussy, too.

Their faces were so eager, I figured why not? Rick was game. He slowly took off my shirt and bra and showed them how I like my breasts to be touched. I was so excited I almost came from that alone. But it was more than the naughtiness of revealing my intimate desires to these relative strangers. For the first time in my life I saw, reflected in their eyes, how truly beautiful I am.

Rick unzips Sara's pants and pushes them down over her hips. Her bikini panties match her bra. I decide this ensemble was definitely chosen for our "interview." Rick hooks his finger under the elastic and pulls. Suddenly Sara is impatient with his slow striptease. She wiggles out of both and kicks them to the floor.

Now we see all of her, her slim legs, her rounded hips and belly. Her bush is neatly coiffed, a landing strip. I catch a whiff of her female musk. Or is it mine?

"Don't you want to spread your legs and give them a good view?"

Sara obeys her husband, flashing us a guilty look. She is very pink and wet down there, but it's the vulnerability of the pose that gets me. Her thighs open wide, she is so trusting of him— and us.

"You want me to show them how you like to be touched down there, don't you? Just like I did our first time in Maui?"

Sara nods shyly.

Her husband's finger finds the sweet spot. She trembles and mews.

Everyone understands that two lovers create so much more erotic energy between them than one person pleasuring herself. But few have the courage to explore the pleasure more partners can bring—an exponential expansion of ecstasy. That night in Maui the four of us made love in the same room, with our own partners, side by side. You might think that's tame—people expect wild orgies—but with that simple act my whole world suddenly felt wider, richer, boundless.

"Do you want to tell them what you told me in the car on the way back from the restaurant, Sara, honey?"

"No, Rick, they might just want to watch tonight." She looks at us through half-veiled eyes. Her hips still move rhythmically against Rick's fingers, which strum her slit like a guitar.

Make me do it.

Her voice has been dancing in my head all evening, but suddenly it's taken on a life of its own. I know exactly what she wants. It's what I want, too.

"Tell us what you said, or he'll stop touching you." That's my voice and I barely recognize the crisp confidence in it.

Sara jumps at my commanding tone as if she's been slapped, then she bites her lip and looks away. But I sense this is all part of the game.

Rick grins. "Don't be rude to our guest."

She moans again. Her pussy is so wet, it seems to sparkle like pink sequins. "Well, in the car...on the way home...I confessed that I'd gotten turned on watching you and Paul across the table in the restaurant. Such a handsome couple, so much in love. I said I wished I could watch Paul show you off to us, teach us what pleased you, like our first time in Maui. And then...." She falters into a sexual sigh.

"Go on," I say.

"I said...I said I wanted to watch Paul make love to you and see what your pretty face looked like when you came."

My stomach tightens, as if her very words have exposed my intimate pleasure to a room full of strangers. But I have to admit I was expecting this, almost hoping for it, the invitation to step across the line from watching to doing.

I glance at Paul. Unsure of what the evening would bring, we promised each other that we would leave the moment one of us felt at all uncomfortable.

"What do you think, Lena?" Paul asks in a low voice. His eyes glitter.

He wants to do it. The choice is up to me.

If I were a good girl, I'd say "no" and mean it. For an instant I imagine being "good." Standing up. Straightening my clothes. Striding to the door in a righteous huff.

And wondering for the rest of my life what might have happened tonight if we'd stayed.

"I guess we start with the shirt," I finally say, attempting a casual shrug. I'm looking at Paul, but I feel Sara and Rick's eyes caressing me like silk scarves.

Unlike Sara, however, I wore a pullover sweater with no buttons for a sultry striptease. Flexing his fingers, my husband takes the bottom of my shirt in both hands and inches it up over my stomach, up over my bra. I raise my arms in surrender. Rick and Sara sigh in unison when they catch sight of the black satin bra.

"And I had you pegged as the prim white lace type," Sara teases. Rick is still stroking her between her legs, but slowly and softly, cruising speed.

I lie back against Paul and he wraps his arms around me. He begins to touch my breasts through the satin, circling and teasing my nipples. The sensation is exquisite, as always, but Sara and Rick's gaze definitely adds a new element of excitement. The ever-shifting light in their eyes—from Sara's approving flicker to Rick's silver-edged hunger—makes my cunt muscles tighten like a fist.

"Do 'the scissors,'" I murmur to Paul.

"Mmm, good idea." He moves to unsnap my bra.

"No, keep it on." Suddenly I realize I want to give this show my own special flavor. Paul always says this bra makes me look like a high-class call girl. Tonight I want to feel just as sophisticated and in control.

Paul doesn't argue. His hands snake around front, and he

begins to show off one of my favorite ways for him to make love to my breasts—by catching my nipples between his middle and index fingers in a scissors-like motion. The sensation shoots straight to my pussy and invariably has me begging to be fucked in seconds flat. I'm already wriggling, but the curiosity in the Porters' eyes stills my tongue. To my delight, in the next moment Rick is doing the same to Sara's breasts. Her eyes pop open and she begs, "Oh, my, keep doing that, baby, it's good."

"Show them our other secret," I say. We may be rank beginners, but Paul and I have come prepared with some surprises of our own.

Paul knows exactly what I mean. His breath quickening, he reaches for the hem of my skirt and draws it slowly up over my thighs.

Rick and Sara gasp when they glimpse the lace tops of the black thigh-highs.

Paul lets his hands creep farther, up and up, so the skirt is bunched up at my hips.

"Oh, my fucking lord, she's been naked under there all night," Sara breathes.

Rick's amber eyes are positively incandescent.

Both stare shamelessly at my lap, although I've yet to open my legs. I decide I like the way their eyes bulge and their lips gape when I make them wait.

But I'm not sure I can take the last step myself. I keep trying to inch my knees open, but they resist me, like heavy doors.

Show us your pussy. You want to, don't you?

Is that Sara's voice or mine? Does it matter now? I wrench my legs halfway open with a jerk. Rick and Sara both jump. Paul puts his warm hands on my legs and waits. I nod. He guides them smoothly open the rest of the way.

"Beautiful," Sara coos.

The cool air licks my wetness. My belly is on fire, and my cunt muscles twitch. Our hosts continue to gaze, entranced.

"Should I show them what you like?" Paul asks, his voice unsteady.

I'm about to nod, but a more wicked vision takes shape in my brain. "No, I want...I want to play with myself while they watch."

I feel Paul's erection twitch against my hip. Rick and Sara are smiling like kids who've been promised triple-scoop ice-cream cones.

Before I can change my mind, I drop my hand between my legs, surprised at how very swollen and slick my lips are. My middle finger finds my clit. I immediately go to town, like I do when Paul is away on business, clawing at myself as if I'm being timed.

Sara shakes her head in delight and disbelief. "She's masturbating in front of us. We made her so horny, she has to masturbate."

"I want you to be a naughty girl like her," Rick replies, pulling his hands away. "Show them what you like to do to your own hungry twat."

With a soft, "Oh," Sara slips both hands between her legs and begins to press her labia together, then pulls them open again, in and out, in and out.

Curious, I mimic her motions. The sensation is incredible—like pinching my clit between two soft, wet pouches of satin. Soon I'm panting, and my thighs start to quiver.

Paul is still dutifully pleasuring my nipples, but I can feel his rock-hard cock trapped and straining against his zipper. It suddenly strikes me as unfair that the girls are having all the fun.

"I want to show them how I suck your cock," I choke out.

Paul's hands freeze. Will he allow it? Will they?

"We have no objection at all," Rick answers, perhaps too coolly.

His answer emboldens me. "And I want to watch Sara suck yours. Come sit beside us so I can see better."

Sara gives her husband a mischievous look. "Maybe you've met your match, darling?"

She takes her husband's hand and guides him over to our side of the room. Rick settles on the sofa a few feet away from us. Sara kneels between his legs and waits expectantly. I scoot off the sofa and kneel between Paul's legs, too.

My husband and I lock eyes. Are we really going to do this? Share our most private act of love with another couple, not one of our fantasies but real flesh and blood?

Paul's lips float in a dreamy smile, but his eyes burn holes into me. His answer is to unbuckle his belt. Together we pull his trousers and boxer briefs down over his knees. His cock springs free and settles like a flagpole at perfect attention. The head is so swollen it threatens to burst like a ripe plum. I don't think I've ever seen him so turned on.

I glance over at Sara. She's staring at Paul's cock, too. In turn I eye Rick's equipment with frank appreciation. His cock is slimmer than Paul's but long and rooted in a tangle of wiry black hair. My pussy clenches.

I take my husband in my mouth. Sara bends to do the same to her eager spouse. Paul sighs and his hips rock up, pushing his cock all the way to the back of my throat.

While I fellate Paul, my gaze inevitably wanders up to Rick's face. He's staring down at me, although his hand is resting protectively in his wife's curls as she bobs over him. And my husband—of course, he's watching Sara at work. Through my lust-dazed eyes, a strange, glowing geometric pattern takes shape in the air around us, stretching from man to woman, couple to couple, sight and sensation melting together.

"I'm getting close. Do you want me to come in her mouth, Elena?" That's Rick. Even when he's getting a blow job, he remains the courteous host.

I pull off of Paul with a smack of saliva. Sara pulls off, too. She waits, a smile playing at her lips.

I lean toward her. "Let's fuck them side by side. But if you can hold off, I want you to let me come first, so you can watch."

She smiles, the perfect coconspirator.

I climb up on the sofa and straddle Paul, positioning myself so his cock slides right in. I begin to push against him, wiggling my ass to give my clit maximum stimulation. Truth be told, Paul and I have always had a special fondness for fucking on the sofa. We do it late at night in the dark, as if we're college kids home for Christmas break, with my parents sleeping upstairs.

Now that we've finally been caught, the consequences are far from dire.

Sara kneels over her husband and sinks onto him with a sigh. Their bodies sway gently together, but it's their eyes that seem so wet and open to the vision of our coupling.

I'm so busy watching their faces, I barely notice that Paul has finally unhooked my bra and is caressing my bare breasts beneath the dangling satin cups.

"Could you finally take that damned thing off so I can see her tits?" Rick growls.

I almost giggle at his sudden rudeness, but the need in his voice turns me on, too. I shake the straps down over my arms and toss the garment to the floor. I square my shoulders, proudly aware that my apple-sized breasts and large mocha nipples make an interesting contrast to Sara's creamy tits topped with raspberries. Rick and Sara stare, their lips parted, as if they're admiring a work of art they made together.

For isn't that what I am? A work of art, enmeshed in the golden web of their gaze, which seems to tighten around my body with each breath? My breasts jiggle as I pound harder on Paul's cock. It feels so good, so hot, I know I am going to come for him—and for them.

Suddenly Sara's hand reaches over and envelops mine in satiny softness. She begins to squeeze in time with my thrusts. My breath catches in my throat. It's as if she's feeding a twisting cable of electric wire up through my arm to bind my throbbing breasts, then twine down into my belly.

"Look at her fucking him, Rick. God I can't wait to see her come," Sara murmurs.

I hear Rick grunt assent but my eyes are fixed on Paul. He is gritting his teeth, holding back for my sake. They're all holding back for me.

Sarah closes her hand firmly around mine.

In the next instant a fireball shoots up my arm, plummets to my cunt and explodes in a shower of sparks. I throw my head back and scream as my orgasm rips through my body. Paul grabs my ass and pumps into me so hard, my knees bounce into the air. We ride the wave together, shamelessly crying out our pleasure.

Sara keeps steady hold of my hand until we're quiet. Then she begins to move her own hips faster and faster. Rick's head shakes back and forth against the back of the sofa, as his eyes dart from my naked torso to his wife, now grimacing in her struggle to the finish. A new warmth begins to flow up along my arm, as if it's a straw drinking in the borrowed pleasure.

Sara's now grinding her hips like a lap dancer. As if on cue, Rick starts to slap her ass. She stiffens and lets out a sexual wail. Rick's hands move faster, wilder, marking her flesh with a flurry of blows. The sofa cushion shivers under my knees, an echo of his desperate bucking.

Paul and I watch with sated smiles.

Then, to my surprise, the heat in my arm begins to throb, and a second orgasm blossoms in my cunt, a slow opening like a fan, followed by languid contractions, as if my own pussy can't quite believe the encore. Paul's eyes widen, and I clutch Sara's hand, like we're best friends in the schoolyard.

After we got back to our bungalow that night, Rick and I immediately fell into bed and made love. It was the best sex we'd ever had to that point. Although I will admit, we've had better since. Going wide lets you go deep. That's what I learned in Maui. I'd love to show you what I mean.

A moment later, I'm already wondering if it was a dream. Did I actually strip, suck my husband's cock and come—twice— in front a couple I'd just met a few hours ago and love every minute of it?

I blink and take a deep breath.

The Porters smile. My husband brushes a lock of hair from my damp forehead and sighs with contentment.

Reality stretches before me, wide, rich, boundless.

ALL'S FAIR

Tiffani Angus

The argument started over something stupid, ridiculous. It was everything and nothing, that argument. Dishes were piled in the sink, bills lay unpaid on the desk, Jay had a lousy day at work, I had a worse one myself. But it escalated from frustrated sniping to yelling to doors slamming and my retreat to a bath to soak and cry and try to relax. He knew where I was, and I waited for him to come to me and apologize. And I told myself that if he made the first move and knocked on the door, I'd gladly say I was sorry first. I just needed that show of regret on his part. When I'm tired and full of self-pity, I need him to forget about himself for a moment and see me—really look at me—and accept the violence of my feelings.

It wasn't until I was toweling off, my skin soft and dewy from the bath, that I heard him shuffle to the door. "My love," Jay said. I froze, towel in hand, water dripping from the ends of my hair onto the rug, and waited.

And all of the promises I made to myself dried up right then, and I knew that I wanted more from him than a hangdog expression and a half-felt apology. I wanted a battle, I needed a release and I was in the perfect position for it, my defenses up because his would be down.

"Open the door," Jay demanded. Then he changed tactics. "Please."

The note of pleading in his voice spurred me on.

"Not quite yet," I said.

"I'm...I'm..." Jay stuttered through the door.

"You're sorry?" I asked, my tone biting. "Took you long enough to get around to it." There, the first volley.

He took the bait. "No, I'm not sorry," he said through the door. "I just came to ask if you wanted me to order dinner."

Anger flared in me as hot as lust.

I opened the door.

And I stood there, naked, more powerful without clothes than with the strongest armor. Jay couldn't help but gape at me, and I dropped the towel to the floor in an invitation. I wanted him to worship me. I wanted to hold that power for a few minutes longer. I wanted to win, so I played dirty.

Cold air wafted in from the hallway behind him, giving me goose pimples and making my nipples ache.

"What?" I asked, impatient, insistent.

I put my fingers over my nipples to warm them a bit.

Jay's eyes narrowed and he opened his mouth to say something, but then closed it again. I dropped my hands and stood straighter, throwing my shoulders back, aiming at him, daring him. One quick glance down at the front of his pants showed that he knew what he was up against.

"I'm done talking," Jay said. "We'll just fight more." He pulled off his shirt and dropped it to the floor, not caring about the little pools of water on the tiles.

"You think we have to talk to fight?" I asked. "What do you—?"

He grabbed me then, his hands around my arms, and pulled me to him and shut me up with a kiss. At first I resisted just enough to show that he wasn't as smart as he thought he was, that I wasn't that easy to win over. But then he slid his tongue into my mouth, bit my tongue, sucked and nibbled my lips.

The size of Jay, his hands, his height, can be overwhelming at times. He has the ability to enfold me, protect me from the world. But even his physical strength and presence wasn't enough when I held the power with one word: no. And I wasn't going to let him win just yet.

Jay moved his mouth from mine to my neck and shoulders and licked the moisture on my skin. I don't know if it was the heat from the tub or the adrenaline from the argument, but I felt almost drunk, unsteady on my feet.

He let go of my arms but I didn't step back, wasn't going to let him think he was gaining the upper hand. I heard his belt buckle and then zipper. When Jay pulled away to take his pants off, I feared a shift. I held the power, not him, so how come I suddenly felt weak? "If you think that this is going to—"

But I didn't finish. Jay grabbed me around the waist with one arm and ran his hand down my body from face to neck, his skin catching on mine where I was still damp, down my breast and across a nipple, then down my stomach and under, where he slid a finger between the lips of my cunt and split me open.

I pushed back one last time, now wanting that apology on principle alone, thinking that I should get that much if he was now going to get what he wanted. But I wanted it as much as Jay...only I seemed to have lost the thread. The room tilted again and I felt by turns angry and hopeful, neither strong enough to overcome the other.

But we both knew that to stop, to talk it out, would just put us back on the merry-go-round. The only way out of this was all-out war.

Jay started the skirmish by picking me up and pushing me against the back of the door, nowhere to go, no way to fight as he grabbed my hands and held them above my head. I could still have said no, but my anger had the better of me and I wanted him to give me something to make up for the fight. I wanted to keep my power, to keep that one little word in my arsenal. I just had to wait for the right moment.

But he never gave me the chance.

I was liquid, my skin cold and hot by turns depending on where his hands and skin and mouth were. Jay licked my neck and sucked the water that still dripped from the tips of my hair. And then his teeth closed around a nipple, and I knew I had to reconsider my plan of attack. The spark of pain traveled down to my clit and I felt myself swell.

When he let my hands go, I grabbed his shoulders and pushed, but that only made him lean into me more. And then his hands were on my hips, around my thighs, and suddenly my knees were up and he went on the offensive and pushed himself deep inside me. I'd barely even touched him, but it didn't matter because I still hadn't said no.

There was no defense against the thrusts that knocked and slid me around. My ass was cold and hot from the bathroom door and his hands and fingers, crushing and kneading and trying to find purchase, as if there were any way Jay could get any deeper inside me.

And each time he pulled out and away and left me half empty and feeling the lack I did what I could to open wider and invite more of him, to shove him into me up to his hips, his thighs, his ribs and shoulders. I couldn't fit enough of him into me to feel completely satisfied.

"More," I demanded, hoping he would understand what I meant, that it would make him even more angry, that I could recapture some of the power I'd had.

Jay looked at me then, stopped completely, cock half inside me. He saw me, and I held his stare, daring him to stop, daring him to keep going.

And then he stumbled, his toe caught on the bathroom rug, and he slid out of me like a missile that's lost its target and I whimpered, nearly cried in disappointment and retreat.

So he kneeled then, grappled with me, awkward, until I slid down the wall and onto the floor, not caring about the mess, my head half on the towel, my right arm pinned against the tub. His hands, hot on my skin, spread my legs wide, bent my right knee over the tub's edge and pushed my left along the floor until my foot hit the cabinet. And he smiled at me then, tight-lipped and trembling, planning his attack, Panzer-tank dick, armor hard and pointed toward the trenches. Instead of a head-on assault, the plunge I was waiting for, he lifted my ass and, elbows down, leaned close and sniffed me from asshole to navel, nose grazing my clit and tongue skimming along the edges of my lips, thumbs spreading me wide. And I lay there, pinned to the wire, held fast in no-man's-land and waiting for the first volley.

Jay flanked me then, twisting around to hide my view across the field, and I felt heat and wet and his tongue battering then smoothing and his whole mouth sucking at my clit and chewing his way around and there was no way to defend myself. I wanted him to keep going and to stop and to ram deep into me again, both at once, impossible to do but necessary. And he knew my longing for the bone-crushing weight of it all, the end to the battle, and he pushed his hand in, two fingers then three, then four, his hand making squelching noises as he rotated and slid it in and out, his thumb free to mash around my clit as he tongued me and rubbed his teeth over the tip. And the tracers sparkled down the bottom of my spine, a delicate light in contrast to the physical brutality of war and I trapped his hand up to the meat of his palm with contractions, bruising and squeezing and letting go and squeezing again and he kissed me then and I tasted my own victory, musky and thick, on his mouth and tongue.

"Is that enough of an apology?" he asked.

"No," I said.

The quick flash of anger on his face told me that I had used my last weapon wisely. "To the victor go the spoils," I said with a laugh and pushed him back down for the negotiations.

NEIGHBORLY RELATIONS

Dorianne

I know I shouldn't be doing this...but oh, how I love to do what I'm not supposed to do, thought Erika as her downstairs neighbor's best friend rolled a condom onto his cock. At least it wasn't Arthur himself, Arthur being the next-door neighbor who had slipped quietly back to his own apartment when it became clear that Erika and his friend—what was his name again?—were hitting it off in the way that results in clothing being removed.

She had promised herself never to fuck Arthur as she didn't want to complicate their neighborly relations, but his friends were still fair game. And here she was fucking his friend, whatever his name was. His name didn't matter as much as his cock did. The member in question pushed its way into her cunt and she gasped a little.

This is a little perfunctory, though, she thought. She'd like him to touch her tits a bit. Sure, foreplay isn't a necessity in a heat-of-the-moment scenario but his hands weren't doing anything important. He was just thrusting; he could at least grab some boob. Actually, the fact that she was even thinking this meant the thrusting itself wasn't that impressive—usually during sex she can't form a thought more coherent than some combination of the words *god, fuck, now* and *please.*

And as soon as she fully realized that she wasn't enjoying herself, he came. Just like that, over and done with. His face squished up, he grunted, then pulled out, tossed the condom aside and went to the bathroom.

Jesus, she thought, *that's the worst lay I've had since high school.* She put her feet back on the floor and picked up the condom before it could spill semen on her carpet.

As unpleasant as the whole experience was, she was still determined to stay on friendly terms with Arthur and all his friends, even the lame lay, whose name it turned out was Blake. A couple of weeks later she was hanging out at Arthur's place with all the boys. They drank a lot of beer and made a lot of crude jokes, which definitely fit into her idea of a good time. But when Blake made a particular remark that was a blatant boast of his sexual prowess she couldn't control herself. She didn't intend to embarrass Blake but she involuntarily snorted, loudly, in reaction to his comment.

Perhaps no one would have noticed her snort if Arthur hadn't started laughing. Arthur, of course, was the only person in the room who knew that she had slept with Blake—other than Blake himself, who now turned her a baleful eye.

"I'm sorry, Blake…" She tried to say something more but Arthur's giggles hadn't abated and they were contagious and she couldn't speak for laughing. Blake was turning a deep shade of pink and their other friends were quickly getting the picture.

"So are you saying you've bagged Blake and it wasn't all it was cracked up to be, Erika?" asked the big one named Craig.

"It was so laughably bad I almost cracked up!" said Erika, then cracked up right then and there. The room filled with laughter and Blake's face turned fuchsia. Finally he could take it no more and he stood up angrily, towering over Erika.

"I was fucking drunk!" he yelled. "I'll show you a good fuck, c'mon, let's go." Erika was astounded, stunned into silence. He took her arm with determination. "Into the bedroom, I'll give you the best balling of your life." The other guys in the room were laughing at this as well, but it wasn't the uproarious laughter of before, the laughter of a friend's humiliation. This laughter was more subdued, more tentative—would she or wouldn't she? Everyone wanted to know. Erika wanted to know herself.

"Well…" she said and paused. In that pause every man in the room caught his breath. "You have a lot to make up for."

"This will change the way you think about cock, trust me," Blake boasted.

"Oh, I think I've had enough cock from you," Erika said firmly, her decision made. "You can make me come—or at least you can try—but the cock stays in your pants." It seemed fair.

Apparently it seemed fair to everyone. Arthur and Craig and the other guy cheered. Erika, stood up, then Blake did as well.

"Hold on a minute. You're not some sort of stealth comer are you?" Blake asked. "If the guys can't hear you, it'll be your word against mine."

"Why do they have to just listen? I'm sure they'd all prefer to watch. Wouldn't you?" Erika asked them, cocky now, excited by the brashness of it.

I've never been in a bedroom with so many men at once before, Erika thought as she slipped her panties off and threw them aside. Then she lay back on Arthur's bed.

Blake started slow. *That's good, this is already more fun than last time,* Erika thought, as his hands lightly brushed her body all over, hesitating here and there to tease a nipple, a lip, an earlobe.

Her eye caught Arthur's as Blake pulled her breasts out from the front of her low-cut shirt. She smiled slightly and he grinned, blushing. Craig noticed the interchange so she looked Craig in the eye and held it steadily as Blake bit down on one nipple and twisted the other. She gasped, but kept her eyes focused. Craig and Arthur and whatever the other guy's name was, she couldn't remember if she ever knew it—the gasp seemed to affect them deeply. They all inhaled at once.

Blake went down and she moved her gaze to her favorite sight—a head nestled between her legs. He grabbed her thighs and pushed them out and up as far as his arms would stretch. Now the appreciative audience could see a full display of her nether regions, pink and swollen. They could see Blake leave lakes of saliva on her labia as he licked slowly all the way up from tip to tip of her crevice. She shuddered as his tongue passed over her clitoris. In response to the shudder the tongue stopped, came back and circled around until she was moaning. Even over her moaning she could hear the heavy breathing from the three boys at the foot of the bed.

Blake's tongue tickled its way back down and unexpectedly plunged into her asshole. She squealed, producing a funny noise. She giggled at her own squeal and laughter erupted from the end of the bed as well. Blake caught the laughter too, and he suctioned his lips around her cooch to laugh directly into it. This vibration cause more squeals, which turned back into moans as he thrust his tongue into her. His thumb, which had at some point migrated down to her mound, inched down farther to rub the hood of her clit.

Her entire physical sensation had moved to the area between her thighs. The only places she felt were where Blake was touching her, with his hands, his tongue, his lips and the rough side of his face.

Her other senses were similarly fixed: her eyes on the eager, lust-filled faces of the three boys at the end of the bed, and her ears on the sounds of sex. The sounds were always her favorite part—or at least one of her favorite parts. Her own breathing and moaning and grunting, the slurpy wet sounds coming from where Blake's face met her pussy and now, for the first time in her experience, the added resonance of three other men heavily breathing.

Both her legs were up in the air and one of Blake's hands was spreading her open to allow his tongue—and the eyes of the onlookers—access to her clit while the other hand worked its way inside her. His fingers thrust into her in the same rhythm his tongue used and her moans turned into screams. She almost lost consciousness for a second—all she felt was pleasure. She forced her eyes open again to see all three audience members stroking erections through their pants. This image was all she needed to come, her muscles tightening around Blake's fingers, her thighs tightening around his head. She held on for an eternity of seconds, then dropped back.

Blake sat back, a smug look on his face.

"So I think I proved myself," he said, and looked back at his friends. His face changed slightly when he saw them, their faces glazed with lust, their erections throbbing through their jeans.

Still panting, Erika propped herself up on her elbows to see that Blake was also visibly aroused. "Now," she said, "I want cock."

Blake whipped his head around, his eyes filled with such delight it made her smile. Before she could even ask, Arthur pulled condoms out from wherever he kept them and showered them down on Erika and Blake like confetti.

"The show must go on," Arthur sang and the boys laughed and clapped each other on their backs, something she'd never seen men do when they all had raging hard-ons.

Blake was already undressed and rolling a condom on his cock which, unlike last time, looked large and hard. Erika's body was taut with excitement. Every inch of skin felt like an erogenous zone. She decided to go big or go home. Her home was only one floor away, but that seemed very far indeed.

"But I don't need just one cock…" She purred and cocked an eyebrow at Arthur, Craig and the boy she didn't know.

They were unsure at first, but Erika knew exactly what she wanted. Once the three had pulled off their clothes, she put Arthur's cock in her mouth and took the other two, one in each hand.

This was what she wanted to be doing. This time when Blake entered her it felt like a totally different man from the time before. It felt like she was being fucked by a porn star. It felt fantastic. She swallowed hard on Arthur's cock, and tightened her grip and sped up on the other two.

It occurred to her that they might not respect her in the morning. This amused her, as much as one can be amused when focusing on four points of sexual contact at once. What benefit was their respect to her? Nice to have, sure, but not significant in any way. No, what she wanted from these boys was exactly what she was getting: a serious gang bang.

Just as she was thinking this, Craig, who had apparently noticed, like a good little lover, that his hand was free and her breast was within reach, started to tweak her nipple. Nameless dude picked up on his cue.

Nothing gets better than this, she thought, her nipples pricking with pleasure, her throat and her cunt and her hands filled with cock.

Blake's ardor suddenly picked up some steam—he lifted her ass up and started pounding into her hard and fast. There was nothing she could do but match his speed with her mouth, sucking hard and fast on Arthur, and with her hands, pulling cocks closer and closer to her face.

She could feel Blake getting closer to coming and she was almost there again herself. She tightened her cunt muscles around Blake's cock, drawing him deeper inside her. She swallowed Arthur's cock all the way down her throat, rubbing her tongue up and down its underside. She looked up at the two other boys, their eyes questioning, hers saying yes.

Blake came first, shuddering into her, collapsing forward into Arthur's back. This forced Arthur a little farther down Erika's throat, even though she had been sure she couldn't take any more. She felt Arthur's jism flood down her esophagus and that made her come too. She came so hard she squeezed Blake's cock out. Craig and the other one were coming too, which just prolonged her own orgasm: each drop of hot wet semen on her face made her convulse again.

They all collapsed, falling over the condoms Arthur had so merrily strewn about. She was touching each of them somewhere. She liked to feel a cock get small in her hand after she had made it squirt. They took a very long time to recover.

She spoke first. "Would anyone else like a beer?" she asked. They laughed and agreed—everyone wanted a beer. They got up and straightened themselves, pulling their clothing back on. Arthur thoughtfully gave her a clean towel from his closet to wipe herself down with.

As they settling into the living room with their fresh beers, she broached her concern. "I decided I don't really care if you respect me in the morning," she said "but let me know if you're not comfy with me coming down and hanging out anymore."

"What's respect got to do with it?" snorted Arthur, which sounded to Erika like a cross between Tina Turner's "What's Love Got to Do With It?" and Aretha Franklin's "Respect." "If you weren't before you are definitely now my favorite neighbor ever."

"Actually," said Craig, "I was really hoping we could do this again sometime. Only next time I want to do Blake's part."

Erika thought that wasn't such a bad idea. She turned to the fourth boy. "And what exactly was your name again?" she asked.

LET ME IN

The Empress

"Let me in, Tom!" screamed Kajol, clutching the clothes Tom had placed in her arms. She kicked at the front door, banging it as hard as she could with her bare heel. The crickets silenced themselves, further chilling the country night air.

Tom quietly answered through the door. "Go home, Kajol. We're done here."

"You can't treat me this way," she implored, shivering in her black lace slip. With a free pinky, she adjusted her saffron panties and noted mirthlessly that Tom had torn the seam of lace in the heat of seduction and rage when gripping down on her hips, pressing her against his couch. The tiny pearls that dotted the flowers in the pattern fell around her feet, and the panties, without the seam's support, were giving way to gravity.

Earlier that evening in Tom's front room, with nothing but qawwali music playing in the background as a greeting, he had hastily disrobed her and himself down to their underwear and moved on top of her on the couch without so much as a hello.

Between breathy kisses, mean little bites on her lower lip and deep prolonged suckling of her nipples through her slip's satin material, he had asked her if he was a good lover. A construction contractor by trade, he sank the large calloused fingers of one hand into her cunt and thrust while with the other hand pulled her hair at the nape. He weighted her arched body with his as she cried with anguish, and waited for her to respond. Panting in the peach-candlelit room of his home, Kajol surfaced from the depths of agony and desire. Caught in a moment of pride as his kind green-blue eyes watched her, she wordlessly stared at him.

Tom's eyes flashed. Temperamental, he perceived Kajol's silence to be cruel. He proceeded to pay her back in spades, bruising her lips with hard, enveloping kisses and whispering harshly into her ear, "You bitch." Grabbing a strong hold around her body with both arms, he ripped her panties off and fucked her with wide strokes. Unable to outmaneuver his wild boorish fucking, she felt his body sliding against hers, his coarse pubic hairs sanding her clit into a raw orgasm. A sharp scream escaped her lips. He looked down upon her and silently came, not revealing a clue of his release other than the swelling of his cockhead inside her. She groaned as another wave of plea-sure washed over her. The final engorgement of his dick as he came inside her was a pleasure in its own right. Gasping for air, her mouth barely reaching out over his shoulder, she held him around his waist and insisted he stay inside her. Firm and gentle like a warning, he bit her on the cheek and pulled away.

Now standing outside, desire cooling in the night air, she yelled loudly for the neighbors to hear, attempting to strike his sense of propriety: "I'm not your prostitute. I have feelings!" She stomped hard on the wooden porch and a smattering of pearls fell around her ankles and bounced away into his shrubs. She clutched her clothes closer to her breasts. It was a cool night, like most nights in the country alongside the redwoods. When it was clear that Tom would not respond to humiliation or her hurt outrage, Kajol padded barefoot, ragged in lace, the mile home to her country cottage down the road.

Over the following weeks, Kajol was listless and short with the clients that came through her office. The San Lorenzo Valley housed primarily white people of lower income level with issues ranging from domestic abuse to meth addiction. As a social worker, she should have shown more restraint, but she found herself unable to grant the slightest compassion to her hapless group. She could not help herself. Despite the humiliation of being cut off from spending the night with Tom, Kajol's pussy hummed in constant anticipation of contact with him. Her desire for him refused to leave her in peace.

Irritability and longing escalated when she occasionally ran into Tom at the farmer's market or the post office. Sometimes Tom would make it a point to find Kajol off guard down some aisle of the food market or behind the blue kettle corn tent at the ice-cream social just so he could wordlessly stare her down. These encounters proved stressful. His gaze impregnated her dreams. He would stare at her from a distance in the tinny gray of her dreams. Some mornings, she would awake to find claw marks on the insides of her thighs and teeny bite marks at her wrists. Her breasts became heavy with want as she found herself carrying the weight of both their yearnings.

Kajol had at first underestimated Tom's androgynous stature. He was slim not like some femme-boy, but wiry and hard like a sharecropper or an apocalypse survivor, his build coupled with a formidable glare and an equally formidable large cock. She wanted to slap him when he pulled these silent staring games on her in public, slap that gaze right off his face and make that unaffected mouth say something, do something to her pussy for just fucking once—but she dared not do it. One time in bed she had slapped him to see what would happen. He did not express the usual shock, protest or arousal other men had. He did not skip a beat in his stroking deeply into her cunt, but his face turned to stone and blanched papery gray. Her blood had chilled and she would never do it again.

Finally, one Saturday morning while Kajol was nurturing a cup of chai spiced with orange peel at a local coffee nook, Tom came in with paper in hand. Impulsively, she sank her nails into her wrist as she jealously watched him converse with the barista. His favorite color seemed to be green and today he was wearing a fitted green plaid button-down under his leather jacket. His pair of jeans seemed a bit worn at the cuffs. It fit the San Lorenzo Valley look just fine except that his dark black hair was cleanly short. He was wearing a belt with an electric blue lightning bolt traversing the length of his waist, and Buddy Holly glasses. For reasons unknown to her, the Buddy Holly glasses hardened her nipples. She shuffled in discomfort. Tom seemed to sense her presence and turned from the barista midsentence. Before turning away with his soy mocha latte to go, he winked at her.

Kajol, a woman born to significantly prudish Indian parents, bristled. Good girls were not to be winked at. Shaking, she said: "I don't think it's appropriate for you to be winking at me."

As he was about to exit, he turned and winked again.

This time she stood up and shrieked after him, "I mean it. A man of your age, winking at me, a young woman, is absur—"

He cut her off with another wink and went out the door.

Kajol grabbed her purse and bolted after him.

Tom's beige Toyota was parked behind the main strip next to the Victorian library overlooking an empty overgrown green lot. He was setting his drink and paper in his truck and was about to settle in himself when he turned around and spotted her. Self-conscious and unsure of what to say, she stopped just a few steps away from him and they both stared at each other. Kajol squinted as she faced the afternoon sun and Tom's glare. She noted that though Tom held a good poker face when he wanted, his hands did shake a little just now. The wind blew a little against Kajol and pushed her unkempt shoulder-length black curls back.

The sunlight brought out hues of gold and red in Kajol's brown skin. The deep richness in her skin highlighted the glint of that yellow gold necklace Indian girls like Kajol were prone to wearing. He could see the outline of her sturdy and graceful legs as the wind licked the hem of her crimson dress.

She absently pressed the folds of her dress downward so as not to reveal herself. He guessed her to be wearing French lace, probably black. Just then, the wind blew the sheathy red dress against her and he could see the outline of her abdomen, her navel, and a bit lower, the cleft of her pussy. His heart clattered to his groin. Maybe she wasn't wearing anything at all.

He raised his eyes to her cleavage, which primly revealed itself from behind her dress neckline. She was glaring up at him. Not to be cowed by her presence, Tom grabbed Kajol by the wrist and pulled her close to him. He found himself sweeping his hand over the front of Kajol's dress. With one movement he cupped one breast and handled the heaviness and the firmness of her and swept across through the indentation of her cleavage to the other one. He marveled at the firmness of her, the sweet buoyancy as he combed his fingers over her tits.

There was a kind of mischief in his eyes as he lightly teased the nipples to excruciatingly taut erections with his thumb and forefinger. He watched Kajol's brow tighten and her mouth open at his gall. She inhaled in disapproval and squirmed against his grip. Before a word was uttered, he closed his mouth over hers, muffling her protest. He locked her mouth in his and kissed her until she gave way and let his tongue explore the soft pink insides of her cheek and lips.

She tasted like orange peel, cinnamon and cardamom. He broke away and nipped at the apples of her wide cheekbones. He slid his mouth to the rim of her exposed cleavage, licking behind the cloth at her nipples. He gave way to a moan as he eyed her dark purple-brown nipples nestled within her dress. She definitely wasn't wearing underwear today. He pried one breast free and when it bobbed into full view, he flickered his tongue and then sucked a mouthful of her tit. He held her, a hand supporting the small of her back; he bit and sucked deeply, rocking her gently into his mouth.

He rifled his hand under her skirt and cupped her pussy and beckoned her body closer. She was slithering wet. With some greed, he shoved a finger at her vagina and felt satisfied of her tightness. Kajol panted with abandon; her hands gripped him around his shoulders, clawing deep into his shoulder blades.

She searched with her cunt for the trace of his hard-on through his jeans. He watched her jaw clench as his coarse jeans pressed into her. He squeezed her outer labia lips together and pulsed them against her clitoris. Heavy lidded, Kajol moaned with the desperation of a dying bird and buried her face in the crook of his neck and absently sucked at his skin. With his other hand he grabbed her asscheek and pressed her gyrating cunt against his erect member.

He kneeled down, hand still in her pussy, pushed her dress out of the way and watched his fingers sink deep inside her. He beckoned with his fingers and kneaded her ribbed G-spot. She gasped and shuddered hard with one hand over her mouth and looked away as though what he was doing to her was too private for her gaze.

Antagonizing her modesty, he roughly parted her legs and stuck his nose into her cleft. He inhaled deeply. Kajol's pussy was always the sweetest: fresh, clean, like fruit. He rubbed his mouth over her engorged pink clit and made sure to run his stubbled chin against it. She shrieked and grabbed his head as if to stop him, but found herself pressing his open mouth onto her clit. She came hard with his fingers digging into her G-spot. Still hoping for another, she ground her pussy against his rasping tongue.

Tom pulled away for a breather, hands on her hips, and wiped his face on her dress, "Goddamn, Kajol. Just wait a fucking minute, will you?" She laughed lustily, leaned back and playfully pushed him back with her heel. He swatted her leg away and undid his trousers. The head of his dick peeked over the rim of his blue boxer briefs. Kajol inhaled softly at his member and found herself gently stroking his penis through his briefs.

Tom's dick stood in attention waiting for her. She tsked, flirted at it and kissed the underside with her eyes open watching. She followed with more kisses and then let the head slip into her mouth. With a firm hold of it in her mouth she licked over and around his head and dipped the tip of her tongue into the opening of his penis tasting the salty come that beaded in drops there.

After generous sucking and kissing at the head, she stopped and looked intently at Tom's dick. He watched her as she spoke not to him, but to his cock. "I like you, it's him I have problems with," she said, and pointed at Tom. She snickered to herself and then looked up at Tom, eyes shining. She stopped and admired his member; it was swarthy with a slight undertone of pink. She pushed at the ridges of his head and firmly slipped the tip in and out of her mouth.

Tom watched her and smiled. Kajol, who was prone to nervousness, lost all sense of decorum when it came to sucking dick. Just a few moments before she had frozen up at his winking, but now out in the open air, albeit an empty parking lot, with very little shelter from a truck door, she sucked slow and steady with relish. She relaxed when it was important, sighing and slipping his head in and out of the side of her mouth with some whimsy and loved to take her time slowly sucking on him. She jabbered to herself with eyes half closed while she let her mouth water over it. He never understood what she was saying when her mouth was full of cock.

She stuck out her tongue under his head and allowed a copious strand of clear precome to run into her mouth. She made kissing sounds at his penis as if to beckon more fluid. She scratched gently over the contours of his balls that were ribbed with desire and took all of him in her mouth, sucking the excess skin of his ball sac and tonguing down the meridian. At this he relaxed. She pressed firmly behind his balls, at his perineum. His knees buckled against her bare tit, scratching her already sucked-sore nipple. His belt buckle scratched a red line at her chest as she drank another sip of his precome. The heat of her mouth was delicious; Tom thought about coming down her throat. He threateningly jabbed the back of her throat, toying with the idea. However, as Tom found himself at the edge of release, he decided he wanted to fuck Kajol in thanks for what she was doing with her mouth.

He pulled his member out of her mouth and rubbed himself against her forehead, her cheeks, down her neck and against her tits. She rhythmically moved her cleavage against his dick, pushing at the head, sometimes looking up at him for cues, and sometimes flicking her tongue at it. He pulled her up and kissed her. She kissed him back in her sleepy way, moaning at his tonguing and the wet grip she had on his dick. Tom pulled away from her.

Kajol's hair was an assortment of curls that leaned to one side and her mouth was wet and swollen from her desire. She was a glossy mess, those scathing, large Indian eyes looking mean and furrowed; she was panting with open lust, fingers at her pussy underneath the folds of her dress and her other hand preventing herself from falling out of the open door of the Toyota. His cock stood on alert, angry at Tom for pulling away from Kajol. Tom wanted to scratch at her, to make her feel the effect she had on him: hear her scream out in raw panic.

Instead, he grabbed the hem of her dress and lifted it off her body. In one zip-slip moment Kajol was standing there in black heels, unapologetically naked. She shivered at his nerve and seemed wide-awake now in her vulnerability and yet she never took her eyes off Tom. He marveled at how she did not look to see if anyone was around. Only an occasional car passed by and Kajol seemed content with the privacy of being behind the open car door. She absently brushed her forearms alongside her body, feeling her own nakedness, watching him.

He wadded her dress into a ball and waved it before her, gauging her demureness. She smiled at him, like he was slow witted, as if to say: "You big dummy, don't you know what I'm here for?" She grabbed at the wad of red tissue in his hand and tossed it to the ground. She kicked it under the truck. She was staring at him. She was measuring him.

Languidly, leading with her hip, she turned around, half mounted the car seat, and leaned into the truck. Her full, thick, apple-bottom ass was up in the air, legs parted revealing the pink slit of her pussy just for him.

"Lay it down on me, Tom. What are you waiting for?"

He placed one foot on the truck's doorstep and one knee alongside Kajol's body. "I don't like your tone with me, Kajol."

He slid his finger from her anus down to the deeper cleft of her vagina, ascertaining his mark. Grabbing the interior door handle of the truck for support, he thrust into her cunt. Kajol screamed in pain and pleasure.

Patting her ass as though comforting a steed, he paused so she could adjust to his width and girth. He rocked his hips methodically in limbo, waiting. She moaned and pulsed her pussy around his dick, bearing down on him with her Kegels to control the discomfort of his size. It had been a month since she engaged with Tom and she had a tendency to narrow in size when not in use. The heat of possession gripped Tom.

Grabbing the sides of her hips, Tom collapsed her body down farther on the driver's seat. Needing leverage to gain access to her G-spot, he had her lying facedown over the seat, removing her comfort and the support of her elbows. Now with her face buried into his newspaper, arms sprawled outward in prostration and ass jacked in the air, he loped in and out of her to agitate another series of orgasms out of her.

Kajol petulantly hammered her fists and muffled her screams into the leather passenger seat. He chided her, "Are you drooling on my leather?" There was a menace to Tom's voice that Kajol knew well. He was kidding and then he was not. She readied herself for a round of punishment. He swatted her ass with the palm of his hand and dicked hard into her. She huffed and screamed.

In her screaming, she found clarity. He could be obsessive or nonchalant about her, driving her wild, confusing her, keeping her hanging some days and satisfying her on others. She knew deep in her heart that this is how he planned it, keeping her desire leashed solely to him. She was screaming herself hoarse. When she caught her breath to speak, her voice seemed hollow, disembodied and distant.

"Was that the best you could do, Tom? Stop fucking around and do it right." She egged him further by spreading her pool of drool around in wide circles on the leather. She talked tough, but she was panting and there was a touch of hysteria in her voice. Tom stroked her body with wide arching sweeps of his palm. Her body reflexively quivered. She flushed red over her shoulders and around her hips and buttocks.

Tom relaxed, groaned at her nerve and her physical robustness. She could take a real thrashing to the pussy, like no other woman he had met before. Other girls were waifs in comparison, unable to handle Tom's stamina, often complaining once he was beginning to warm up. She was always challenging his complacency, what he thought he knew about women. Nothing was safe with this girl.

Internally, he could feel her G-spot swell. "I think you're ready, Kajol," he murmured. He lay on top of her, almost losing his footing, and kissed her between her shoulder blades. He reached down underneath her with one hand and pressed into her lower abdomen to prime her for the round of deep orgasms he was about to lay onto her. He hammered her. She fought his grip and squealed. With his other hand, he pushed down between her shoulders to control the angle he needed to rub her G-spot. He breathed deeply, forcing himself not to come at her moment.

Then it happened.

All cries of desire and pain, all the screaming, wrist-biting, scratching, panting, huffing, thrashing, seemed childish and stupid. Deep within her, Kajol rattled off countless deep moans. She could not remember anything. She came in waves. How many times was she coming? Forty, a hundred? She was not all quite there to be able to count. When she came to it was just for the moment to ask him to stop. Her G-spot was inflamed and could not produce any more. She could feel Tom come inside her. He released with a short cry, but this was irrelevant to her; nothing seemed real, not even Tom.

Time slowed; her brain seemed to shut down on her. Tom scooted Kajol into the passenger seat. She did not look at him or even notice that he was in the car handing her red dress back to her. He pulled her toward him and she sluggishly brought herself to hang her arm across his chest.

"Kajol," Tom began, slowly kissing her nose and parted mouth, "am I good lover?"

Kajol forced herself through a haze of sleep to look up at Tom, with his green eyes: sweet, dangerous, lovely. "Yes, Tom. The best lover."

LOLITA

Zahra Stardust

Lolita has lovers in almost every country of the world. Acquiring them is a fetish of hers that developed—initially at least—quite unintentionally, and rather spontaneously, and has somehow become a trend that she finds no immediate desire to escape.

Now Lolita is sitting on a couch opposite a man in a hostel in Tehran. He is watching her eat watermelon that is wet and heavy like a swollen clit. The juice is leaking down her chin and she is spitting out the seeds but they are landing on her top, already carelessly stained with juice, or on her bottom lip.

He is watching her curl those lips into a half smile to the side of her mouth, which is a bleached pink, and how somehow this makes her cheeks glow. He watches her undress him with her eyes, lazily exotic in a way that is impossibly beautiful.

Lolita is terribly attracted to the man sitting opposite her. He is nearly twice her age and they are both excruciatingly aware of this. He is unbearably good-looking and is making her feel slightly light-headed and dizzy, and so she just keeps talking and eating and occasionally stops to drown him in languid, sleepy smiles.

They end up in a teahouse, where he is counting the number of sugar cubes she is using to drink her chai. She is up to six and hasn't seemed to notice.

"You've got nice feet."

She has taken off her socks and shoes that were both dripping from the snow, and her toes are cold and almost purple. He reaches out to touch them.

She looks at him in bemusement through smoke rings from the *qualyan* and turns up the corner of her mouth. This is the first time he has touched her and she hears her breathing splutter. She sucks hard on her sugar cube and feels her teeth rotting.

"Thanks."

"I love the color you've got on your toes..." He gives an affectionate wink.

She laughs at his contrived charm. Her nails are black, with remnants of a dirty aqua underneath.

She puts her hand on his thigh under the tablecloth. He pretends not to notice, and watches her, all cold toes and dreamy smiles. He just wants to hold her. Instead he drowns her with the sensation that she is sinking through ice.

Giddy and giggling like a couple of school kids, they are handing over *rials* for the room. By now it is nighttime, and they have accidentally spent the entire day together, both so magnetized that they forgot to leave.

As they stagger into the hostel she is strangely kaleidoscopic. He is watching her shoelaces trawl in the dirt and her wiping her hands on her pants, decorated with pink and yellow safety pins.

He puts her money away.

"It's all right, I've got it...."

And then, "I've got more money than you," as if it was an afterthought.

"Nah, I have almost a thousand bucks."

She grins.

He looks at her out of the bottom of his eyes in the most condescending but ultimately sexy way, and she grins. She knows that he probably has a house somewhere around the world; she knows he has been working for the last twenty years. She knows that they both know this; she knows that the conversation has only served to remind them that she is but a dandelion in the mouth of a tiger.

"I've got it."

She lets herself be persuaded, and they make up a story about how they are engaged and have been together for years, despite having met for the first time yesterday. *Thank god they didn't ask for a marriage certificate,* she thinks. Just in case, she twists one of her rings over to her left hand and suddenly feels uncomfortably ashamed of what they're doing, in this beautiful country that's not their own.

She can no longer look the hostel staff in the eye. The scenario is so ludicrous and perverse that she can feel herself blushing. Then he bumps her shoulder with his as if she is his younger sister. This makes her smile continuously for the next ten minutes.

Now he is watching the way she sits cross-legged on the bed but lying down so her head is hanging off the edge, bluntly and vulnerably exposed. He is watching her aqua and black nails and how she speaks to him upside down in the mirror. She can feel him watching her play with her hair.

He wants to open her up and extract from her all the kinds of idiosyncrasies you find out after sex. He wants to open her up, like a flower, like an oyster, like the pretty little thing she is, and just have her. He wants to flip her over and over again like a pancake and devour her. He wants to grab that neck and strangle it in some kind of predatory urge while he fucks her hard up the arse.

This is no secret to her.

She turns onto her side and looks at him, the pillow between her cheek and the back of her hand. He listens to the sound of her throat sucking in air. He looks at her, and she blinks in slow motion. In that blink is the sensation of her ruthlessly and impulsively squeezing his balls and kissing him firmly on the mouth. She blinks again. He waits for each blink as if it is the biggest come-on you could ever imagine.

She's young enough to be my daughter, he thinks.

He's old enough to be my father, she thinks. Just.

Both are not sure whether to be disturbed or turned on by these libidinous thoughts that seem strangely and inescapably and mind-bendingly arousing.

She is lying now with her head in his armpit, and he is finding the most wonderful pleasure from watching her shiver and recoil and nuzzle into him, achingly cold and feline. He is calling her "sweets" and things that make her feel delicate, and stroking her fingers with his thumb, wondering if she notices. She does. Of course she does. Her breathing is tortured because of it.

He looks at her through half-shut lids. The way this looks is incredibly perverse in the best kind of way. The way she looks at him is up through the top of her eyes with her lids wide like butterflies, and the way this looks is innocent and greedy and lasciviously suggestive, as if she is daring and begging him to have her at the same time.

Every now and then she slides her hand underneath his shirt

and into the belt of his pants and feels that muscle at the base of the spine and the top of the butt. She can feel his belt buckle hard against her left hip bone and in this there is a novel intimacy that is almost unnerving. This sexy, cocky guy whose ego she knows how to please, and tease—she is tracing her nails down his side, she is waiting for him to flinch, grow ticklish; she is waiting to feel his breathing stop.

Men are singing and giggling and yelling in Farsi in the kitchen upstairs. There are prison bars on the windows. The bed is squeaking and rattling all at once. They are dizzily spun out from the kerosene heater.

"Romantic room, huh?"

She is playing with his earlobes and has her legs wrapped high around his chest. He is thinking that maybe she is flexible and that could come in handy.

"Do you do yoga?"

"Mm…yeah… Why?"

"Just thought you were the type."

"The type…"

She closes her eyes, and lets him build up some yogic schoolgirl fantasy of her back home.

He holds her head, sunken into his shoulder cavity, with his whole hand. His fingers rake up the back of her neck and he cradles her skull as if he were holding up the head of a newborn baby. He is wrapping her hair around his fingers in a way that she can never be sure that he won't pull her head to the side and let his teeth sink into her neck. He is craving her in a way that is all at once protectively paternal, instinctively territorial and fantastically erotic.

She is tracing her finger down the vein that runs fat through his bicep.

"What, so you've never been fucked up the arse?"

His eyes are incredulous, and she can swear his mouth is watering.

"You've never tried the back-door thing?"

She just smiles like a kitten.

"I was always up for it." Casual.

He nearly chokes. Then he grins as if all his Christmases had come at once.

"Really?"

By now his voice is almost growling with temptation. She just smiles darlingly like some innocent kid, crippled by his lust for her—that savage, wordless lust. She just lies there and smiles, and fantasizes about being violently corrupted.

She is conscious of her slightness underneath him, conscious of her youth beside him. She indulges in it like it is her ace of spades. She is holding his bicep in her hand like a football, pawing at his neck with her nails like a panda bear, and sneaking bites at the lobes of his ears. His chest hair smells of soap and she knows he probably washed himself thinking of her, like she did when she let that water stream into her cunt so she would be sweet and tasty.

He is leaning over her now and looking at her. He has his hands on her stockings and she is thinking how she would give up everything she owned if only he would rip them off her. And all she does is blink again, with that loose, amorous smile.

And so he kisses her. Because he knows she wants it. And of course she does.

He touches her, and she is humming like an engine. She is purring like a motor. She can feel his breath in her ear, and before she knows it he is pressing her against the wall in a way that makes her body freeze and melt simultaneously. When he kisses her she feels dumbly serene, and she just keeps grabbing him by his hair and pulling him into her and impulsively kissing him hard and wet on the mouth and telling him that he is very, very sexy. He likes this.

"Your pussy's really warm."

"Hmm..."

"So you're really only twenty?" He grins.

She laughs at the progression of his thoughts. Kisses him. And shrugs. "Older guys do it for me."

He kisses her back: wet, impassioned.

"Well, I usually go for older women but I guess I'll make an exception for you."

She scoffs and then laughs. Like he was doing her a favor.

They are struggling in the single bed with a dirty hostel blanket and a sleeping bag that keeps sliding off toward the heater.

"Fuck. I've melted a hole in your sleeping bag. Sorry."

Her head is full of the scent of him, and prurient, wanton thoughts, and all she can feel is a burning in her womb and the sensation of her unchaste hands all over his moist skin. She can hear his breath quickening in fierce arousal and the thrill she gets from this is incredible.

Suddenly they are pushing two single beds together, and she is climbing on top of him like a dominatrix; she wants to watch him in tantalizing torment underneath her. He is bemused by the spectacle of her seducing him, wonderfully turned on by the spectacle of her seducing him: this small, young, hungry sexual deviant. She wants him to lust after her like she's a schoolgirl. And of course he does.

She is up to her neck in his body.

He is telling her how fabulous her black nails look around

his cock, and in her dumbly happy state she is absorbing him like some kind of drug.

Soon he is standing at the foot of the bed in all his nakedness with a hard-on and that Amazonian fish-tail necklace. For a moment he looks like he's just stepped out of maximum security, walked into the bedroom and been handed a condom.

She is being taken to the beds and laid down diagonally across them, like a patient, and explored. He is strong enough to just lift her up or onto him at his whim, like a little fuck doll. The kicks she gets from this are indescribable. She is glued to the image of his head buried inside her, and his tongue tormenting her. All she can think is, *I love that mirror.*

The window is locked ajar with his shoe, and the breeze is making her nipples erect. So he kisses them with heavy, hot kisses. The breeze is giving her goose bumps down her navel and down her thighs. And so he kisses them with heavy, hot kisses. But this just makes her shiver even more. He has laid her flat on her stomach and has her wrists trapped beneath his calloused, iron hands.

Her earthy, vegan, hippy self has learned to miraculously— momentarily, at least—dispel the fact that he is a meat-hungry hunter, whose politics she protests against back at home. Desire crosses all boundaries, it would seem.

He bites her neck. He bites her neck again, and again. He bites her neck slowly and just hard enough that it makes her wince. His mouth is open wide enough to almost suction her whole neck. And every time she winces she feels her body contract, waiting for his teeth to break her skin, and then she melts. She breaks into a smile and waits for him to bite again; wet, lusciously. With each bite is the tickling of his heavy breath, and his spiky stubble and his soft pillowy lips. She is laughing and wincing and melting in harmonious succession. And in between each bite she cannot breathe at all.

Now all she can feel is his hand around her neck like a noose, clamped, from behind. She can feel this and his fingers pulsating and squeezing and the sensation of her hands out to her sides and pressed flat against the bed. The way she feels is like a blindfolded doll.

The way she feels is like a naked prisoner forced against a wall. The way she feels is violently submissive. This sensation of helplessness is erotic like you would not believe. Her face is pressed hard against the bed as if against glass and this makes it hard to breathe. She is almost blue and yet she wants to drown under that hand, she wants to dissolve beneath it. She wants him to suffocate her.

There is mascara all over the pillow.

She wishes she'd cleaned her ears in that cold shower this morning, as he seduces them with his tongue.

Her undies are being pulled aside with one finger, and for a moment she thinks she is going to be fucked like that, and then they are yanked down around her ankles with his feet. She is undone by this, utterly and totally and irreversibly undone.

He has his finger lubed with spit and tracing up toward her arse.

"Are you into this?"

She is being flooded with all the urges of her sexual being and is surprised she can articulate anything intelligible.

"I'm into you."

So now he has his cock deep inside her arse and two fingers up her cunt and she feels lavishly open like she would let him have her body in any way he wanted. She is being molded like a piece of putty and she wants to scream but all she can manage are random guttural releases. She can hear his breathy male growl that sounds as if he's been holding his breath up until now and that makes her feel wonderfully delirious.

He has lifted her and positioned her and bent her over backward in so many different ways that she is beginning to feel like an elastic Barbie doll. She reaches up and pulls him into her and she can feel him, sticky with sweat, his collarbones bumping against hers.

And all she can think is, *Spank me.* She can hear the words over and over in her head like a gasping metronome.

Then they are lying on the bed and the breeze from the window is drying their sweat. She has her head in his armpit again but this time so she can inhale him and smell how she has made him sweat down the ravines of his body. She is peeling off flakes of her black nail polish and sprinkling them over his chest. Just to be annoying.

With her head to the side, through one eye, and through her hair, she can just see their silhouettes in the mirror. She is lying, small, vulnerable, cold toed and beautiful. Her jewelry is lost somewhere under their clothes—her hair elastic, her underwear, his jeans from Brazil with their pockets weighed down with a million things and looking as though they should have a *Crocodile Dundee* knife attached to the belt—or somewhere under the bed.

They have bitten each other's lips so many times that she is sure she can taste blood in her mouth.

She smiles and thinks of strawberry fields and bruises.

THE GOURMET

Chaparrita

Bella went to Mexico for rest and relaxation yet ended up spending most of her time sucking cock.

Bella was a world traveler with a gourmet palate. She was a petite and vivacious dark blonde with a winning smile, sharp green eyes and round natural breasts and hips that made men drool. She was curious, an adventurer with her bag slung over her shoulder and a camera perched in front of her face to capture the gorgeous scenery. She was the kind of woman who was most happy with a man fucking her pretty little mouth.

Day One
Bella staked out a spot on the beach by ten a.m., just as the sun crested the mountain and hit the slice of sand in front of her hotel. Her winter skin was as pale as milk against her cherry-red bikini, the one with little black polka dots, the one that barely covered her breasts. She lolled in a beach chair, slave to the rays; big, glamorous-looking sunglasses covering her eyes and a huge

straw hat shielding her head. Bella smiled at the young Mexican who'd brought the beach chair out for her. He perched on a rock about thirty feet away, acting indifferent when it was crystal clear that he just couldn't take his eyes off her curvalicious body. His brown-eyed stare played over her like the sound of waves on the shore: light, happy and sensual. Bella inhaled the smell of salt, her fruity sunscreen, the young man's attention.

Then the damn kitchen came to mind. She'd finally taken time off. It had been a year since her last vacation. She was the executive chef at an upscale bistro in New York, which was a pressure cooker—pun intended—of a job. Bella managed two sous-chefs and a team of prep cooks, dishwashers and other cooking minions, mostly men. It was hot, sweaty work and she presided over the kitchen like a self-assured queen at court, not because she was a bitch but because when people ate at her bistro, they expected the best. And that's what she was. She'd worked her way up starting as a teen, proving herself in the urgent kingdoms of talented yet egomaniacal male chefs who'd treated her as if she were a little girl who couldn't handle the knives and fire. Now when she entered the kitchen in the morning, activity stopped. Her team grew instantly silent and everyone would turn, saying, "Good day, Chef!" She had cookbooks, TV spots, and she was known by just one name: Bella. She could *more than* handle it.

Bella's thoughts stayed pleasingly culinary as she mused about the recent lamb-tasting menu her bistro had featured. Lamb chops, lamb medallions, lamb-stuffed ravioli. She imagined herself gnawing a leg of lamb the way she liked it: large, gamey and with the bone in.

Bella softened, melting into the shimmering heat. Finally the images of the kitchen slipped away like so much seaweed on the surf. She took a thirsty sip of mango soda, wiggled her toes and turned to the pages of a steamy read she'd brought along for fun, something she'd picked up on a whim one afternoon in Brooklyn.

Victoria moaned wildly as his thick, pulsing cock entered her hot, tight pussy. Thorne had been after her for days and now he would make her his, conquering her with forceful thrusts. She rode him like a fine stallion, bucking on his huge member...

Oh, please, Bella thought. *How cheesy can you get? Pulsing cock? Huge member?* But despite the language, the story was getting her seriously wet, her pussy swelling and blooming with arousal, becoming liquid. She licked her lips and read on. Soon her skin reddened and not just from the tropical sun that was a little much for her delicate complexion. She rose from her chair, feeling sweat trickle between her breasts, and headed to her room to cool off for a few minutes.

Once there, Bella threw herself on the blinding white bed and lay under the whirring fan, listening to the ocean until she didn't feel so light-headed. It was partly the heat and partly her suppressed appetite for sex, rising to the surface and demanding to be acknowledged *now*. How long had it been since she had really *tasted* a man—at least for more than an awkward fuck in the wee hours of the morning after the restaurant closed? How had she let the restaurant overshadow her bedroom? Bella grabbed her book with one hand and greedily caressed her clit with the other, reaching underneath her bikini bottoms and moving in slippery circles. She was just...getting...close...when there was a knock on the door. She ignored it until the mysterious guest banged again, more forcefully, and called, "*Señorita*? I bring to you something."

She adjusted her bathing suit, took off the chain and opened the door to find the young Mexican man, carrying an ice-cold fruit soda in a bottle with a straw. His white T-shirt and pants contrasted beautifully with his dark skin, his short and solid frame like a barrel. His hair was short and bristly. It made her want to rub his head.

"I think you get too hot," he said, offering the bottle. She clasped his wrist, meaning to unnerve him, and sucked on the straw. Both the sparkling drink and feel of his smooth skin were delicious. He surprised her with a rash move, a suave gesture, wrapping a strong arm around her waist and kicking the door shut with his foot.

"Hey," she said, hesitating for a second.

Then she fell in, thinking, *Oh, fuck, I don't want to act like I don't want it because I do, I want it*, kissing him, letting him grab her ass and slip fingers into her bikini top to tweak her upturned nipples. He bent and latched on with a groan, kneading her breasts as he sucked. She pushed him away, breathless, and they stared at each other like animals facing off. He backed her toward the bed and she sat down hard, looking up at him with big coy eyes. He had tasted of limes and something honeyed. Alcohol, and before lunch.

"What you want? Tequila?" he asked, teasing, jutting his hips forward in a nasty, cocky dance move.

She shook her head slowly, holding his gaze.

"Cerveza?" he asked. In response, her hand boogied up his thigh to his crotch, where a juicy-looking cock strained. She lowered her head and ran the tip of her tongue up its length, softly nipping, licking, pinching him through the material. He sighed.

"Ai," he said. "You need verga." She nodded, dazed, wanting nothing more than to service, submit, be stuffed full; to wrap her lips around this strange young cock in her face. And with that, he pulled it from his pants and she plunged her mouth over it gratefully and longingly, groaning loud as if she were in intense pain. Her hand wrapped the shaft like a hug and slid up and down as she sucked the tip, then took all of him deep into her throat, then trailed down to his balls, sniffing, savoring something like cumin, like vinegar, a spicy smell that made her moan. She suckled and devoured and blissed out in a ravenous feast of cocksucking, cock against her tongue and throbbing in her hand. His hips moved against her, his rhythm growing faster as he grabbed her shoulders for balance. He wasn't the biggest and he wasn't the most experienced but damned if she minded. A passage from the dirty book flashed to mind:

...Thorne fucked her glossy mouth, almost choking her with his rock-hard member...

The man's cock jumped, grew stiffer and he unloaded roughly into her mouth, just like she knew he would, and she came, not from touching herself, just from the intense pleasure of the man's dick in her throat, just from his salty liquid stream. Bella drank down every drop, shuddering with her own climax, And took her time licking him clean from balls to tip, purring to herself. Then she sent him away. Adios.

Day Two
The floodgates were open. She was hungry for more.

Bella woke with a grin. After sleeping in and enjoying a leisurely brunch and cinnamon coffee on her porch, scribbling menu ideas in her notebook, she wanted to see what the town had to offer. Her guidebook promised old-world charm and modern shops.

She strolled next to the ocean, toes in the sand, a long green dress floating about her ankles like mermaid sea foam. Everywhere she saw tourists and locals walking, sunbathing, or enjoying conversation with drinks. She grinned at a warm memory of the glance she'd caught in the mirror of herself attached to the young man's crotch, his hand tangled in her hair as he pushed her onto his erection. Yes. The boy was a nice appetizer. Somewhat rustic, like a robust slice of brown bread and village cheese. Filling yet incomplete, leaving the patron eager for more complex flavors. For the meat.

Idly she wandered, distracted by her blow job dreams, not noticing the men noticing her flow by in her green dress. Not noticing the intense lust her hips sparked as they swayed down the street like mariachi music.

The unassuming gallery captured her, wooed her with color, the white walls teeming with paintings of vines and flowers and animals. It looked like Bella felt: alive and wet with life. She should have come to Mexico long ago! She stretched her arms overhead and stopped in an open courtyard, admiring a massive canvas that depicted hot-pink bougainvillea draping over a wall and cracked stones, each flower shining with detail, each leaf perfectly outlined. She could almost smell the sweetness of the blooms.

"Wonderful, isn't it?" A slim man with a cultured accent approached.

Bella agreed. "Love it. It's just pulsing with energy." She faced the man and saw he was fortyish, with a teeny bit of gray in his lush black hair. His body looked taut, feline, and his stance said he was certain of himself. He wore a yellow shirt tucked into jeans with a belt. The way he leaned toward Bella said he was attracted.

He extended a hand. "Juan Vargas. This is my gallery."

"Bella."

He held and kissed her hand, his eager warm lips pressing her skin way longer than socially appropriate. He was sizing her up like a fruit at the market. Bella plucked at her dress strap, sensing her nipples growing firm. "Sorry for the cliché, but I couldn't help it," he said, his eyes oozing into her cleavage. She wore no underwear and no bra and it felt wonderfully free, free as the breeze. She wondered if he could tell. She wondered if he knew his naughty lips had woken her pussy, which now felt slick under the slip of a dress. Bella shifted her hip and thought about a hard hot fuck.

"You don't sound Mexican," she said. "I detect a hint of…"

"French. My mother is French and my father is *Mexicano*. I went to university in Paris but the primal beauty of my father's country seduced me back."

Birds called from somewhere outside.

"Show me what else you have in the back room," she said.

His ass looked fine leading the way down the hall, and she admired it like a lion regards the juicy haunch of a gazelle before the kill.

As soon as the door shut, he was on her like green on guacamole, aggressively taking her breath away with his skilled tongue—hint of chili!—and hands, tugging her dress up to tap the sweet spot. Before he could reach her sodden pussy though, she sank to her knees on the wooden floor, taking him down with her. She was the queen. She called the shots.

Juan hummed joyfully as she tortured him with each slow click of the zipper, springing his wide cock from the jeans. He leaned back on his elbows on a stack of books and she lapped, sucked, fucked him with her lips, tongue and throat. She couldn't get enough cock in her mouth, pressing her face against his thighs to take every inch. How could anyone ever get enough of the power, the fabulous rush? Of giving a man pleasure this way? Of the visceral force of having your throat filled like the round notes of a song? Juan's face beamed ecstatic, much like someone eating one of her creations, caught in delicious ecstasy. She opened wider to fit all of him in, released him out, took him in, tugged on his balls, worked his length with the flat of her tongue. On all fours in the dust, surrounded by beautiful works of art and rolled canvases, Bella was in heaven, moaning and rubbing her rosy pussy with her hand while blowing a stranger.

...there on the floor with her mouth full of cock Victoria realized she was a whore, a dirty, filthy, wanton little whore who loved to fuck and be fucked...

"You're not getting off that easy," he rasped. If he only knew! "Now I take you." She squeaked as he shook her off and moved behind her, holding her round hips tightly as his dick danced into her waiting cunt. Her edges were so fat and puffy that they enveloped the rigid shaft. He screwed her hard, fast, expertly, like a man who knew women, who knew how to use a cock, slapping her ass with the palm of his hand and making her cry out, her pussy grabbing and the climax rippling out like a seismic wave. Bella felt tears in her eyes and realized he was climbing, ramming with abandon, words in French and Spanish spilling out.

"*En mi boca! En mi boca!*" she cried. *In my mouth*. She didn't mean to let him take control but he did and she'd let him. His cock slid between her lips—she had so missed it being there—and she tasted their juices together, sour lemon and savory oregano. Her hand flew and her tongue tickled the ridge behind the head of his cock and sent him hurling over the edge. A river of come washed into her mouth and she moaned around him, clawing his ass with her hands to hold her mouth against the deluge.

She had the bougainvillea painting shipped straight to her bistro.

Day Three
Eat, lounge, swim, nap.

Controlled New York Bella had given way to open, Tropical

Bella, the dial on her finer senses cranked to the hilt in the moist, fragrant air. Her thighs were sore from dancing, her mouth from sucking. She stepped onto the balcony as the sun went down, naked and dewy from a shower, feeling potent, surveying the blue and pink of the sky. She'd broken out, somehow, with all the sexual release she'd allowed herself. She felt complete. Satiated. She'd taken her sexy back! Now she wanted to take her badass self out to celebrate and indulge her palate instead of her libido.

The concierge made a reservation for her at a restaurant where the chef was known for his exquisite creations. Rocking to *banda* music on the radio, Bella pulled on a tight, pink sundress that celebrated each and every curve, applied a hint of mascara and lip gloss and admired the goddess in the mirror.

...she had opened her most secret flower and was glowing from inside out...

At the restaurant:

"A little *regalo* from the chef, *Señorita*," her waiter said, passing her a tiny bite in a silver spoon: the *amuse bouche* to whet her appetite. Mouthwatering, perfect *ceviche* puckered her lips with its sour snap. She followed it with a sip of a fabulous, nuanced wine that smacked of apricot and grapefruit. The restaurant was a mix of metro and Mexican, like something that belonged in a bigger city. Each course was better than the last and Bella was surprised with the chef's panache and inventiveness. She savored every single bite, taking her time. As she enjoyed her dessert wine, she felt the loose satisfaction of a stunning meal, wriggling her hips under the table and thinking about the other kind of satisfaction she'd experienced on this trip.

A beautiful wild man interrupted her reverie and she lost her composure, spilling a bit of her wine on the table. Embarrassing. He was standing in her personal space, reddish curls springing from his head, jeans, beard, broad shoulders, flip-flops. "Gomez," he said. "I hope I was able to impress you tonight." He smirked at the effect he'd had on her.

This was the great Mexican chef? No way.

"Bella," she said. "From New York." She waited for the usual reaction but he made no sign he recognized her. "The sea bass and *ceviche* were superb, ah, and I was blown away by the way you used cilantro and anise. And the raspberries with the caramel..."

"You must be a chef!" he exclaimed, laughing loudly. "*Riqu-isimo*. Come, come see my kitchen!" Excited, he took her by the hand and led her into a bustling hive of jumping fire and bubbling pots, his staff in smart uniforms while he looked like a hippy off the street. She was thrilled. She felt at home.

Gomez dipped a ladle into a great soup pot and brought it to her lips.

She swallowed. He watched.

"Marvelous. I'm not sure about the saffron, though," she said.

"Of course this sauce must have saffron," he said, waving his hands and scowling.

Bella put her hands on her ample hips. "Saffron overpowers the other ingredients, in my opinion." She smiled: just trying to help.

Gomez became quite still and smiled back. He said, "Please, let's discuss this further in my office." They wound through the kitchen into a small, cool space, shutting the door behind them. Bella looked forward to some hearty chef-to-chef conversation. Instead, he exploded.

"Who are YOU to come and tell Gomez that his SAFFRON doesn't FIT?"

"Don't you KNOW who I am?" she said. "Bella. You know, Bella?"

He waved a hand dismissively. "*Woman*. A little woman who thinks SHE can tell ME how to cook!" He shoved all the papers off his desk in a rage, muttering angrily in Spanish, pacing around with his hands gripped behind his back.

She took a sharp breath as the papers fluttered to the floor around them. It was indeed his kitchen. His territory. But now he'd pissed her off. "And your sea bass could have been cooked thirty seconds longer," she spat, tossing fuel on the fire.

"Whore!" he cried.

"*Pendejo!*" she countered.

He slapped her face.

She slapped him back.

He shoved her over the desk, snatched her dress up and pressed an amazing erection against her bare ass so suddenly her breath caught. He pinned her against the wood of the desk and growled, grinding his hips like a madman. She felt intense fear, then shock, then the overwhelming urge to have Gomez inside her.

"Take me, bastard," she moaned. "Just fucking fuck me."

"Oh, I will fuck you," he snarled, undoing his jeans and slamming into her wet cunt with a cock as wild and gorgeous and uncontrollable as he was. "Bossing me around. Whore. Slut. *Pendeja.*" With each word he thrust deeper, harder. The sounds of their angry jungle fucking were raucous. She thought the entire restaurant might be listening. She didn't care. Each time his cock pumped into her she cried out.

"Like it?" he said, swiveling his hips, making her feel even more delicious. If that were possible. Bella was dizzy with pleasure. She only managed to moan *Mmmmmm*.

He pulled out. "On your knees, *mujer*," he said, lowering himself into a big leather chair. "I'm going to fuck your lovely mouth." His cock was magnificent and thick, roped with veins. It looked proud and strong and like the starring dick of her fantasies. She took his balls into her mouth, tasting his funky sweat, nuzzling her nose into the moist curls that matched the reddish ones on his head. "Suck," he commanded, murmuring approval as Bella's lips engulfed him totally, worshipping his masculinity through the root. They both whimpered.

He was hard, as hard as she'd ever felt a man. He tasted of chocolate, the brine of the ocean and the freedom she'd been searching for all her life but never found. Not until she entered his kitchen. His cock begged for her touch and she swirled her hand on his shaft, watching his green eyes watch her. The fat, spongy head felt especially good penetrating her mouth, stretching her, traveling the full length of her throat over and over.

The only sensation was cock. Cock and the desire to please and be pleased by this man.

...as he took her, she experienced absolute ecstasy and finally unleashed the wild woman from her cage...

She moaned in protest as he moved away, holding her hand out for his cock. Their eyes locked and wordlessly he bundled her into his lap, now as gentle as he was rough before. Her cunt sheathed his cock and their tongues met for the first time. *This wasn't what she was expecting.* Slowly they intertwined, kissing insatiably, his hand directing her ass up and down his shaft. She ran both hands into his red curls and held his head as her mouth traveled his lips, cheek, forehead. As she kissed him, he grasped the neck of her dress and ripped it open, taking her breasts in his mouth like a starving man, licking from one to the other, one to the other, wetting her entire chest. Tasting her. Fucking her.

No: *making love* to her.

He made her come.

And then held on tight as she came again, riding his cock and calling to God.

Gomez came in a hot burst, pulling out and splattering her thighs. They held each other, panting. He grinned and ran a finger through the white sauce spilling down her leg and pushed it into her mouth, following the finger with his big, soft lips.

Bella dissolved into a puddle of bliss.

He kept his hand on her cheek, narrowing his eyes. "And how do we taste?"

"Perfect," she said. "I wouldn't change a thing."

THE MAGICIANS

Valerie Alexander

It's a night of symphonies and snow. You and I are at a holiday party and we're avoiding each other. This old brick house used to be the grandest in town and you and I once knew it as well as we knew the bounce of a soccer ball, the boredom of study hall; back in those high school days when we knew each other. Now the host hobbles from room to room on artificial hips and the wine cellar has long gone empty and the library books go unread. It's a different kind of haunted house. I'm studying the worn oriental carpets and dark red wallpaper, the grandfather clock. There's a ghost in this house and I'm here to invoke it.

"Alison." The host, Russell, takes my hands with the benevolent welcome of a town patriarch. I was his son's girlfriend in high school. "Thank you for coming. If only D.J. could see you. It's been what, almost fifteen years?"

"Thirteen. It's too bad he couldn't make the party. I did hear his company is doing really well."

"He seems to have the golden touch. Did you see Trey is

here?" Russell's wrinkled eyes are shrewd as he glances at you. No doubt he's noticed we haven't spoken to each other, despite how inseparable we once were. You were D.J.'s best friend. "He's living in Boston now, like you. I don't know if you two kept in touch."

I don't let myself look your way. "No, we haven't talked since the summer after graduation."

The caterer gestures him away. I sip my vodka tonic. You're talking to Russell's lawyer but you look at me across the living room in every natural pause of the conversation. We each knew the other would be here tonight. Neither of us brought a date. You're as tall and broodingly handsome as you were in high school, with those slight circles under your pale eyes that I always thought made you look so debauched. You're giving me looks of pained nostalgia. I'm thinking of everything I wanted from you in high school and how I only got it once. How I want to hear that I'm why you came to this party. That I'm the ghost who's haunted you.

A tray of miniature éclairs circulates. The grandfather clock strikes ten. I haven't long to act, this party won't go all night. These guests are older. You and I are the youngest guests here and we're not really so young anymore, are we?

Except that Mother Nature may be acting in my favor. "It's really getting bad out there," says the local orthodontist, peering outside. This is something said about five dozen times a winter in our New England hometown, but there's a certain lunar blue to the landscape that says the blizzard gods may indeed descend on us tonight.

"I'll bet the garden is already covered," Russell muses. "Alison, will you take a look out back and see if the cars looked snowed in yet?"

"Of course." This gives me the chance I've been waiting

for all night, and I slip down into the dark hall that leads to the east wing bedrooms. Or as it was called when we were in high school: the kids' rooms. D.J. and his brother not only had massive bedrooms but their own den, where we all hung out unsupervised. The rest of us were so impressed. "My mom would never let me have a guy in my room," I said to D.J. the night we brought in German beer and a dirty movie. That was the night I lost my virginity, D.J. pumping away on top of me trying not to come while I bit my fist from the raw sensation of being split open. (What was really erotic about that night: showering when I got home and feeling alive between my legs for the first time; the heat and tenderness of my cunt and the cool water on top of it.)

Now I stand in the chilly dark hall that smells not of musty closed-up bedrooms, but of lemon furniture polish and money. Russell's maid service still cleans down here. I wonder what they think of these lost boys' bedrooms, their soccer balls long since put away, their bureau drawers emptied of cleats and uniforms and underwear. I know what I would do were I to enter this wing in the middle of the day: finger myself on the red-blanketed sleigh bed, my bare legs wide open just like one time right before graduation. I did it then because D.J. asked to watch, but I was pretending he was you.

I snap on the old hall light. Its weak illumination shows up faded wallpaper, two closed bedroom doors and the dark entrance to the den. My feet hesitate. I don't really believe in ghosts. I believe in the corporeal body. But an odd hulky shape looms in the shadows and I'm almost afraid to go closer until I realize I'm looking at an old console TV, complete with a VCR. Everything is the same. The green couches, the leather ottoman. The fake bar in the corner.

"Alison."

Your voice sounds deep and languorous just like it did in high school. That's why I don't turn around, because I'm picturing the way you looked at eighteen, your sand-colored hair and lanky six-four frame. You were always laconic and mysterious, even when we were kids. Aloof and dreamy, you seemed like a different species from the braying teenage half-wits in our gym class. You barely seemed to notice the girls who mooned after you; I wanted to fuck you partly just to pierce your reserve, to see your hazel eyes change when I swallowed your cock or knelt on the bed and spread my ass open for you. I was a volcano that spring I was eighteen, and I knew that if D.J. was the teenage boyfriend I'd leave behind, you were becoming the man who could ignite my sexual future.

You step up behind me and peer into the dark den. "It's exactly the same."

I don't step aside so you can go in. I want you to touch me to get by. Once again, though, you're in the role of D.J.'s best friend instead of in the role of pursuing me.

"I didn't think Russell would have changed anything," I say. "It's not like D.J. or his brother ever visit."

You're standing so close to me. My heart is a rabbit trembling in a prison. I want you to slide your hand under my dress, this winter-inappropriate dress I wore tonight with just this hope in mind. Because then I would know you were remembering a forest keg party so long ago when you followed me into the trees and put your hands up my shirt and groaned into my ear with such heartfelt longing that my heart and my pussy seemed to merge into one thudding organ of need. Just for a moment, and then you were gone.

"Weird being here," you mention.

No kidding. Now I know you're off your game.

I look at you over my shoulder. While most people's eyes give them away, with you it's your mouth; your full gorgeous mouth, with your teeth set in your bottom lip just like when you fucked me into a frenzy. I used to secretly watch your mouth in calculus all senior year and on that day I finally had you, you bit your lip with every thrust. I was flattered by your savagery until I realized D.J. was fingering your ass and driving you crazy, too. But I was too delirious to care.

I make my own banal mention: "I've been wanting to come back here all night."

"Is it your first time? Since...then?"

I smile. "Yes. Since 'then.' Yours?"

"Yeah. D.J. and I didn't..." His voice trails off.

I figured as much. At first when they stopped talking to me after our threesome, I thought it was a boys united thing. But the silence extended between all three of us and when D.J. went off to college without saying good-bye, I realized how serious the breach was.

"I get why it ruined your friendship with him." My voice is embarrassingly strained. "What I never understood is why it affected things with me."

You look ashamed. "Alison, come on. It wasn't okay back then for straight guys to—do that. And you were there. I think kids today are more flexible about that kind of thing...."

We both smile because we're not old enough to talk about *kids these days!* And yet so much has changed in the last thirteen years and so have we, sort of.

"I get it now. He was your best friend, I was your best friend's girlfriend. I just..." I look up at you again but can't say what I need to: that no sex, no man, not even the threesomes I tried to duplicate it with, have ever come close to the supernova burning through my body that day. That nothing has equaled the electricity of when you watched me and D.J. have sex and then your self-control collapsed and you crawled over both of us with a groan of pure hunger.

"The butler did it in the library," says someone with a nasty laugh. We turn. Russell's lawyer is standing in the hall. "Christ, this old house is spooky. I'm waiting for Vincent Price to walk out of a room. What are you two doing down here, anyway?"

"What are you doing here?" you ask with that cool imperiousness that was able to intimidate even teachers once. The teenage girl in me quakes.

"Oh, Russell sent me to get you. D.J. showed up, if you can believe that." He rolls his eyes and heads back down the hall.

It's amazing how many thoughts can travel through my head in the move from one room to another: *This is like fate; wait, it's been thirteen years, he's going to look different. I wonder if he'll think I look different; wait, he's almost thirty-two, he's got to be married. Rich guys like that always have the trophy wife. I wish he wasn't here, he's going to ruin everything.*

You and I walk into the living room side by side like a couple. That's how it feels, at least, when D.J. turns around from his father's friends and his eyes go first to you, then me. He looks good in a polished executive way, his black hair tucked behind his ears and his eyes harder than ours. Apparently owning a successful software company is wearing. You guys greet each other like the old high school friends and former teammates you are: smiles, claps on the back, banalities.

"Alison." Now his eyes fill with real emotion and he hugs me. So there's still a little twinge after thirteen years, that's nice. I look over his shoulder for a date. He seems to have come alone.

"This is quite a surprise. Your father said—"

"I flew in from Singapore." He probably doesn't intend this to sound braggy, the globe-trotting executive, but it reminds everyone of the differences between us. "So! You look great! You both look great. What have you...been up to?"

His voice fills with strain and we all know why: that last "you" targeted us as a couple. He doesn't know that we haven't spoken since that day. So I tell him.

"I can't speak for Trey because this is the first time I've seen him since then."

He goes silent. Then laughs awkwardly. Neither of you are looking at each other. Did I ruin it? I don't care. There's been enough silence.

"I need a drink," I announce. "Why don't we all catch up?" And that's how I take the night into my hands.

We wind up on the green settee in the library. Okay, we don't wind up there, I deliberately steer us there because it will force us to all sit together, me in between you and D.J. He has a hand on my knee and keeps squeezing it, yet it feels avuncular and his eyes are mostly on you. Maybe he's gay now and you're the only one here he cares about. Maybe this is going to end in forty-five minutes with awkward good-byes and separate walks through the falling snow to our cars.

"I'm never here, I usually just fly Dad out to wherever, so I thought this would be the ultimate surprise," D.J. is saying. "It's been years since I've been back. And nothing ever changes. Small-town America." He shakes his head and sips his drink.

Small-town America. Like you and I are some younger version of Ma and Pa Kettle, waiting to be regaled with stories of corporate royalty. Your eyes meet mine and we understand each other perfectly.

"It's great that you've done so well," I say. "No wife, no girlfriend?"

"Ha, no. I work day and night. Don't know anyone who'd put up with that."

"Your room is exactly the same," you say. "The den, at least. Alison and I were just down there."

This startles D.J. "You were? Oh." Tense laugh.

"Your old TV is quite the relic," I tell him. "The whole place is like a time warp."

D.J. peers over at the bookcases like he's trying to read the titles. He's struggling with something. You and I both scent it the way we scented each other's craving when I walked into the party tonight. For him to be this ungraceful, this unable to smooth the way into neutral safety, says he's ours for the taking if we want him. Or rather, if we want each other in this specific, bittersweet nostalgia.

Russell pops his head into the room. "Look at the three of you," he says. "Just like old times." He smiles emotionally. "You know, it's really coming down out there. I don't know if you're going to be able to dig your cars out. Alison and Trey, you're welcome to spend the night if you wish."

D.J. looks down at the carpet. Maybe he wishes we would go. Maybe he wishes we would take his clothes off and gag his mouth and do everything we did to him that day and more. Next to me, you lean into my leg just enough to send an electric current through me.

"That would be great," I say. And then the three of us are traveling through an oriental-carpeted wormhole to the past.

You don't turn on the lights and so the bluish glow of the blizzard spills through the windows. We're not in the den. We've gone into D.J.'s bedroom instead. It's empty tonight, devoid of the dirty socks and glass dragon bong and soccer trophies I remember. The big wooden sleigh bed is tightly made up as it never was back when D.J. and I would practice our adolescent love here. This is the bed where I first slept naked with someone. The den couch is where I choked over my first blow job, D.J.'s cock huge and ungainly in my mouth. That couch was probably the site of your first blow job, too.

"I think the lightbulb has blown," D.J. offers, which is a ridiculous justification for not turning on the lights, but we can keep it dark for him. The room was brilliant with sunlight that July day when we fucked and tongued and came on each other, all three of us eighteen and so earnest in our lust, and utterly clueless of how beautiful we were. Thinking about this makes me want to see you both naked. We've crossed into our thirties now; we're seasoned, skilled and graceful, in theory. The cartographer in me wants to map the fault lines of our transitions.

But you're the one who starts it. You push D.J. down on his bed with easy dominance and pin him there by the biceps. He shifts in what seems at first to be a protest until he arches his back. You're smiling kind of evilly. Oh, Trey. So this is who you turned into, a masterful bastard who knows how to command. I kneel on the bed next to D.J. and he looks up at me with hope and hunger: I'm still wanted here. That's gratifying. Together you and I undress him until he's naked and open for the taking. His chest is broader now, a line of hair on his stomach that wasn't there in high school. My smooth, snake-hipped soccer player is gone.

He twists toward me to kiss my pussy through my dress. My nipples fill with heat but he stops as you step back from the bed and take off your clothes. You do this in a way that says you mean business. D.J. watches you with the same voracious fascination I'm feeling, and I understand then that you probably dominated his adolescent fantasy life as much as you dominated mine.

You take out your cock like it's a weapon. It's as smooth and long as you are, and you stroke it rather menacingly. Then you spread D.J.'s thighs wide as if you're going to fuck him just like that, no condom, no lube.

But you don't. Instead that sinister smile returns and you trace your swollen crown around his balls, up to his navel, then crawl on the bed and taunt his mouth with it. "So what have you been doing all these years, D.J.?" you ask with a laugh. But it's rhetorical. We're about to find out who's been doing what all these years.

D.J. is breathing fast. He looks up at me, as if for permission. I scratch one fingernail across his bottom lip.

"Fuck his mouth," I tell you.

Your cock splits his lips and plunges all the way in. He chokes a little and you laugh and pull back, just enough for him to adapt. I adjust his head, slightly jealous that I won't get that first dusty taste of your dick freed from its confines. You straddle D.J.'s face with an academic frown, moving this way and that until you find your rhythm and settle into a controlled and steady groove.

You look up at me. A wry smile spreads across your face. We look at each other for a few wordless moments of confirmation, and then you reach forward to take off my dress. I unhook my bra for you because I remember how my tits were the first thing you went for at that party in the woods where you finally let me know my insane crush was mutual.

"Oh, Alison," is what you say right before we kiss, a devouring, cannibalistic kiss that's too full of teeth and jaw to be good in the romantic sense, but is everything I need. Your hands are on my tits, my hands are in my underwear. D.J. struggles to keep sucking you as you pull me close. This is what I've wanted tonight, for years, forever. You naked and consuming me.

Brusquely you run your fingers over my slit, then smear the wetness on my nipples before sucking them clean. Then you push me on my back next to D.J. and bury your face between my thighs. Your tongue feels strange and invasive and warm on my clit, an incubus robbing me of control. I'm almost scared to succumb to this hot new glory rising through my blood. All I can think of is getting your cock inside me, your arms around me, but my nerves are tuned to such a fever pitch that as soon as you work two fingers into my pussy, I lose it for real, coming and flooding the bed.

We didn't do this before. It was so spontaneous that day of our threesome, the way you climbed between my legs to replace D.J. and fucked me with an urgency he never had. I looked up at you in such a frenzy of white heat that I could have sworn there was a halo around your beautiful face, but then I saw D.J.'s face next to yours, kissing your jaw and biting your neck. You were groaning and I realized both of us were making you come. You collapsed on me and kissed my collarbone but D.J. took over—pulled you up by your neck and forced you on your knees to suck his still-hard cock.

I lifted up on my elbows to watch, too amazed by the incredible sight of my boyfriend getting head from my secret crush to demand that you come back to me. I'd never seen you submit to anyone before. So it was half miraculous to watch you hesitate and struggle over his cock. Gradually you found your method and started sucking him fast and tight—and I watched your face change from intimidation to power as you took D.J. under your spell deeper and deeper with every stroke, your own cock growing stiff again. You didn't even let him come. Instead you pushed him back onto me and as he pumped out his final throes inside me, you took his ass from behind with a determination that I wanted so badly to be aimed at me.

"I love you." Someone says that now in the dark. And your mouths are occupied so it must be me. You kiss my inner thigh like a kiss of secret code. Strange how we know each other so well after a silence of thirteen years. Strange we didn't know how to move toward each other back then. But all that is past as you pull your cock away from D.J. and crawl up my body to kiss me for the first time, hot and slow and real. This is the dream I dreamed at seventeen, at twenty-six, in bed with men who weren't you. Your mouth and body covering mine until my every sensation is you.

Snowflakes tumble and blow past the windows like pale blue furies. In their light, D.J. looks confused and a little disturbed as he curls next to us. I pet his hair and he looks back at you.

But you're looking at me. Because I've always been your dream, too. This is the unlikely coda to a symphony performed only in our minds. You bite my throat and nipples, run your tongue around the undercurve of my breasts, squeeze my ass with a groan. Doing everything we didn't do before, every wish that was lost to chance and shyness. Your whole body is shaking as I take your cock in my hands. Touching you feels almost hallucinatory and I want to stroke and lick you from your eyelids to your toes. But your hard dick is sticky with precome and throbbing against my fingers in a plea for relief, so I open my legs.

In one swift move, you pin down my arms and push all the way inside me. Your thick cock fills me completely until I feel almost impaled. This is really happening. Euphoria electrifies my every cell.

"This time I'm not going to stop," you say in my ear, so D.J. can't hear. I wrap myself around you as tight as I can. And that's how we correct destiny, your wet skin slapping mine and your face floating in the dark like a mirror. Your back rises and falls, muscles straining under my fingers until I can smell every animal part of you. Without warning, you roll me onto my stomach and fuck me from behind until I'm moaning and crying into the mattress. Your fingers pull and slap at my ass, every thrust of your hips driving me deeper into a delirium of memory and bliss. I slide my hand underneath to stroke my clit until my spine feels split open with heat and I dissolve into a wet, shuddering second orgasm.

The snow will descend all night. We're fucking in a museum of lost love, an exhibit of the futility of preservation. An icy draft from the windows drifts over our skin but we keep bucking, clawing, riding each other. All our potential watches from the dark as we immolate the past with every thrust. Here in this house of stopped clocks and paralyzed rooms, our bodies are burning like live wires and we won't stop, resurrecting fate like magicians of time.

ABOUT THE AUTHORS

VALERIE ALEXANDER is a writer who lives in Arizona. Her work has been previously published in *Best Lesbian Erotica, Best of Best Women's Erotica* and other anthologies.

TIFFANI ANGUS is a spec-fic writer working on a creative writing PhD in London. A graduate of the 2009 Clarion Writers' Workshop, she has previously been published in *Strange Horizons* and was long-listed for the British Fantasy Award.

JACQUELINE APPLEBEE (writing-in-shadows.co.uk) is a writer who breaks down barriers with smut. Jacqueline's stories have appeared in various anthologies including *Best Women's Erotica, Ultimate Lesbian Erotica, Surrender* and *Best Bondage Erotica*. Jacqueline has also penned *An Expanded Love,* a romance about multiple loving.

CHAPARRITA is the pen name of an author whose first novel is forthcoming. She has a fiery passion for sex, writing, travel, yoga and anything juicy that stimulates the senses. Her erotica has been featured in Clean Sheets. She's lived and loved around the world, but currently calls the hot and sticky part of the U.S. her home.

ELIZABETH COLDWELL (elizabethcoldwell.com) lives and writes in London. Her work has appeared in numerous anthologies from Cleis Press, Black Lace, Xcite Books, Circlet Press and Total-e-bound among many others, and her story "Heat" was included in *The Best of Best Women's Erotica 2*. "The Nylon Curtain" is dedicated to Adam.

DORIANNE is a writer working in literary fiction, erotica and nonfiction. You can find recent work in *The Mammoth Book of Threesomes and Moresomes,* and on sexlifecanada.ca. In 2011 she will have an avant-garde short story with sexual themes published in the *Mad Hatter's Review.*

THE EMPRESS lives sequestered in a small country town near the redwoods in California. She works as an event coordinator and is currently pursuing her masters in social work.

OLIVIA GLASS is a writer of erotic fiction. She lives in the Midwestern United States. More at oliviaglass.com.

K. D. GRACE lives in England with her husband. She is passionate about nature, writing, and sex—not necessarily in that order. Her novel, *The Initiation of Ms Holly* is now available. She has had erotica published with Xcite Books, Mammoth, Cleis Press, Black Lace, Erotic Review, Ravenous Romance and Scarlet Magazine.

KAY JAYBEE (kayjaybee.me.uk) wrote *The Perfect Submissive, Yes, Ma'am, Quick Kink One* and *Quick Kink Two* and *The Collector*. A regular contributor to oystersandchocolate. com, Kay also has stories published by Cleis Press, Black Lace, Mammoth, Xcite and Penguin.

TSAURAH LITZKY is a widely published writer of erotica. Her work has appeared in the *Best American Erotica* series eight times, the *Mammoth Book of Best New Erotica* four times and in many other books and publications. Her erotic novella, *The Motion of the Ocean,* is part of *Three the Hard Way,* a series of erotic novellas edited by Susie Bright.

LOUISE LUSH is a writer, editor, blogger, filmmaker and online pornographer. Since 2000 she has managed a stable of adult websites for women including MsNaughty.com. She also co-owns ForTheGirls.com, and regularly writes and edits stories, reviews and articles for the site. She lives with her husband in a small Australian town.

SOMMER MARSDEN (SommerMarsden.blogspot.com) is the author of *Lucky 13, Base Nature, Hard Lessons, Learning to Drown* and many other novels. Her work has appeared in nearly a hundred erotica anthologies. She currently writes for Excessica, Xcite, Pretty Things Press and Ellora's Cave. She also runs her own almost-invisible-teeny-tiny-press December Ink.

REMITTANCE GIRL (remittancegirl.com) lives and works in Vietnam. Her novels are published by Republica Press, a number of her short works appear in Cleis Press anthologies and a collection of her short stories is available through Coming

Together. She grows orchids, enjoys watching people have sex, and writes about it.

ZAHRA STARDUST is a Penthouse Pet, magazine centerfold, award-winning striptease artist and Australian pole champion intent on spreading love around the world from upside down. A proud feminist stripper, Zahra abandoned a legal career in favor of taking her clothes off in public, and has stirred up Australian politics as a candidate for the Australian Sex Party.

DONNA GEORGE STOREY's (DonnaGeorgeStorey.com) adult-only tales have appeared in over a hundred journals and anthologies including *Best Women's Erotica, Best American Erotica, Penthouse* and *X: The Erotic Treasury*. She is the author of an exotic, erotic novel, *Amorous Woman* which was based on her own experiences living in Japan.

AMELIA THORNTON is a very good girl with very bad thoughts, who lives by the seaside with her collection of school canes, a lot of vintage lingerie and too many shoes. She enjoys baking, hard spankings and writing beautiful naughtiness, and definitely likes both cola cubes and jelly babies.

ROSALÍA ZIZZO is a hot-blooded Sicilian whose work has appeared on several online sites and in various publications. A former teacher who never lets her progressive multiple sclerosis get her down, she holds a BA in comparative world literature from U.C. Davis and now lives with her husband and daughter in Sacramento, California.

ABOUT THE EDITOR

VIOLET BLUE (tinynibbles.com, @violetblue) is a CBSi/ZDNet columnist, a *Forbes* "Web Celeb" and one of *Wired*'s "Faces of Innovation"—in addition to being a blogger, high-profile tech personality and podcaster. Violet has nearly forty award-winning, best-selling books; an excerpt from her *Smart Girl's Guide to Porn* is featured on Oprah Winfrey's website. She is regarded as the foremost expert in the field of sex and technology, a sex-positive pundit in mainstream media (CNN, "The Oprah Winfrey Show," "The Tyra Banks Show") and is regularly interviewed, quoted and featured prominently by major media outlets. Blue also writes for media outlets such as *MacLife, O: The Oprah Magazine* and the UN-sponsored international health organization RH Reality Check. She headlines at conferences ranging from ETech, LeWeb and SXSW: Interactive, to Google Tech Talks at Google, Inc. The *London Times* named Blue "one of the 40 bloggers who really count."

More Women's Erotica from Violet Blue

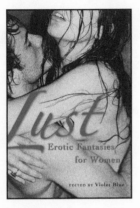

Lust
Erotic Fantasies for Women
Edited by Violet Blue

Lust is a collection of erotica by and for women, a fierce and joyous celebration of female desire and the triple-X trouble it gets us into.
ISBN 978-1-57344-280-0 $14.95

Best Women's Erotica 2011
Edited by Violet Blue

"Every single story is layered top to toe with explicit sex—hard and wet and mean and sweet, flowing with love and fused with characters who finally feel like us, with no apologies..." —from the Introduction
ISBN 978-1-57344-423-1 $15.95

Best of Best Women's Erotica 2
Edited by Violet Blue

Lovingly handpicked by Violet Blue, those erotic gems have been polished to perfection by the bestselling editor in women's erotica.
ISBN 978-1-57344-379-1 $15.95

Girls on Top
Explicit Erotica for Women
Edited by Violet Blue

"If you enjoy sexy stories about women with desirable minds (and bodies and libidos that match) then *Girls on Top* needs to be on your reading list."—Erotica Readers and Writers Association
ISBN 978-1-57344-340-1 $14.95

Lips Like Sugar
Edited by Violet Blue

Sure to keep you up past bedtime, the stories in *Lips Like Sugar* will arouse your appetite for something truly sweet.
ISBN 978-1-57344-232-9 $14.95

Ordering is easy! Call us toll free or fax us to place your MC/VISA order.
You can also mail the order form below with payment to:
Cleis Press, 2246 Sixth St., Berkeley, CA 94710.

ORDER FORM

QTY	TITLE	PRICE
_____	_____	_____
_____	_____	_____
_____	_____	_____
_____	_____	_____
_____	_____	_____
_____	_____	_____
_____	_____	_____
_____	_____	_____

	SUBTOTAL	_____
	SHIPPING	_____
	SALES TAX	_____
	TOTAL	_____

Add $3.95 postage/handling for the first book ordered and $1.00 for each additional book. Outside North America, please contact us for shipping rates. California residents add 8.75% sales tax. Payment in U.S. dollars only.

* Free book of equal or lesser value. Shipping and applicable sales tax extra.

Cleis Press • Phone: (800) 780-2279 • Fax: (510) 845-8001
orders@cleispress.com • www.cleispress.com
You'll find more great books on our website

Follow us on Twitter @cleispress • Friend/fan us on Facebook